"I don't need

Sam regarded his da

They thought Shelby was a nanny!

"Of course you don't," Shelby said, earning her a look of reluctant interest from the child and a glance of grave annoyance from the man.

That wasn't exactly *I am not a nanny.*

"You're a city girl, aren't you?" Sam asked. His voice had a gravelly tone to it that felt as if it was scraping across her skin. And not in an unpleasant way. Best not to let him know that!

"I prefer to think of myself as a woman," Shelby said. *Especially around him.* Something extraordinarily adult was swirling in the air between them.

Sam Waters cocked his head at her. "Woman," he said, his tone flat. "Noted."

That was not *exactly* how she wanted him to notice her. "I'm from New York," she said.

He nodded, as if this was not entirely unexpected, and not a good thing, either.

For some reason, the lines were blurring. It actually felt as if she *had* arrived here as a nanny, not looking to him to provide his ranch for a sixty-fifth birthday party.

Winning Over the Brooding Billionaire

Cara Colter

Recycling programs
for this product may
not exist in your area.

ISBN-13: 978-1-335-59659-8

Winning Over the Brooding Billionaire

Harlequin Enterprises ULC
22 Adelaide St. West, 41st Floor
Toronto, Ontario M5H 4E3, Canada
www.Harlequin.com

Printed in U.S.A.

Cara Colter shares her home in beautiful British Columbia, Canada, with her husband of more than thirty years, an ancient crabby cat and several horses. She has three grown children and two grandsons.

Books by Cara Colter

Harlequin Romance

Cinderellas in the Palace

His Convenient Royal Bride
One Night with Her Brooding Bodyguard

Blossom and Bliss Weddings

Second Chance Hawaiian Honeymoon
Hawaiian Nights with the Best Man

Matchmaker and the Manhattan Millionaire
His Cinderella Next Door
The Wedding Planner's Christmas Wish
Snowbound with the Prince
Bahamas Escape with the Best Man
Snowed In with the Billionaire

Visit the Author Profile page
at Harlequin.com for more titles.

Margo Louise Jakobsen
1948–2023
Beloved.

Praise for
Cara Colter

"Ms. Colter's writing style is one you will want to continue to read. Her descriptions place you there.... This story does have a HEA but leaves you wanting more."

—*Harlequin Junkie* on *His Convenient Royal Bride*

CHAPTER ONE

SHELBY KANE SLAMMED on the brakes, and the tiny car skidded to a halt. For a moment frozen in time, the leaping deer was so close to her front windshield that she felt as if she could see each individual hair on its shoulder and stomach.

She closed her eyes, held her breath and braced herself.

Nothing happened.

She dared to open her eyes. The deer bounded away through tall grass the color of wheat, though it was spring. As she watched, the animal—with the same graceful effortlessness with which it had cleared her car—sailed over a barbed wire fence. It paused and looked back at her, eyes liquid, soft, deeply brown. One ear twitched and then it trotted off, winding its way through a herd of fat, oblivious cattle.

She had never been so close to a wild animal. The truth was, despite the extraordinary beauty of the deer, she hoped she never would be again.

The experience had been an unwanted challenge to her decidedly new driving skills.

Her heart still racing, Shelby got out of the car, leaned on the fender and drew in deep breaths of sun-on-grass-scented air.

She took in her surroundings with a mix of awe and trepidation. She had never been this close to a real live cow before, either. The humongous creatures, separated from her by only the thin wires of that fence, seemed, thankfully, disinterested in her.

She was in the Foothills Country of Southern Alberta. Nothing could have prepared her for the immensity of the land, the endless sweep of the grass and the undulating hills that looked as if they were covered in suede. The Rocky Mountains, brilliant against an endless blue sky, loomed in the near distance, peaks craggy and snow-capped.

Though it seemed impossible, the mountains appeared to be the same distance away as when Shelby had started down the numbered range road. When her GPS, at the turnoff from the main highway, had instructed her to go sixteen kilometers—a measure that, as an American, she was not totally familiar with—she had thought it would put her right in those mountains.

She had pictured herself, white-knuckled, on a narrow, winding road that had unforgiving rock on one side and steep, water-gushing ravines on the other. The Mountain Waters Ranch was her destination, after all.

But no, many flat, straight kilometers later along the dusty gravel road, she seemed no closer to the mountains, and certainly there was no ranch in sight.

She was a city girl, through and through, most recently calling New York home. Though her past lifestyle had allowed her to experience more wonders in the world than most people could even dream of, she had never experienced anything like this.

Rugged beauty.

Endless space.

And an almost terrifying sense of acute aloneness.

Where was the nearest person?

Taking one last look around, Shelby got back in the car. Her GPS told her she had only traveled ten of the sixteen kilometers.

She was somewhat grateful she'd opted for the GPS feature in the rental, instead of a bigger vehicle, though at the same time, she was so aware that her *new* life required her to weigh such choices: bigger car or GPS. The tiny economy car may have fit her admittedly limited budget, but it certainly did not align with the first impression she wanted to make.

She glanced down at her clothes. She'd chosen a classic tailored pair of dark teal slacks and a matching jacket, with a colorful silk blouse underneath. All were designer, as were the shoes, a three-inch spike heel that might not be exactly appropriate for a ranch—or for driving, come to that—but that boosted her five-foot-four height to five-foot-seven in a way that had proved irresistible. A practiced eye would know her clothing choices were not on trend anymore, but how practiced an eye would anyone have who lived on a ranch?

Speaking of first impressions, she adjusted the rearview mirror and took stock of the things she could control.

Her hair, while no longer colored and cut to perfection by Frederique's on Fifth, remained one of her best features. It was naturally honey-colored, and fell in a thick and shiny wave to her shoulders. Looking at it critically, Shelby was pleased with the result she had achieved herself with a blow-dryer and a curling iron. She even wondered if the extraordinarily expensive Frederique had ever actually improved it.

Her eyes, brown flecked with gold and green, still looked wide and startled from her encounter with the deer. Her lashes looked luxuriously thick, and she allowed herself to be newly amazed at how mascara that fit her budget seemed to do just as good a job as the fifty-dollar Epais brand she had preferred in the past. Ditto for her budget lip gloss.

Budget, she thought, not without a familiar surge of astonishment, as she put the mirror back the way it had been and started the car.

As the only child of billionaire business mogul Boswell Kane, Shelby had been raised breathing the rarefied air of the extraordinarily wealthy. She had grown up in family homes all over the world—Paris, Lisbon, London, George Town, Los Angeles, New York—though *family* and *home* would not be accurate descriptions of any of those houses. Each was a mansion, with multiple pools and media rooms, staff quarters and manicured grounds. Each missed the "hominess" mark by about a million miles.

Her mother, Jasmine, had died when Shelby was ten, and even at that young age, She had recognized her father was in some way trying to make it up to her. Her every whim was indulged. There was not a single thing she had ever wanted for.

Shelby had lived the lifestyle of the rich and famous that everyone dreamed of: private jets, fashion events, exclusive designers, spas, parties. She had skied the Alps and scuba dived the Great Barrier Reef. She had been on photo safari in Africa. She had dined with royalty and been backstage with the most well-known bands in the world. She had been to the Oscars and the final game of the World Series.

Had she even appreciated what she'd had when

she'd had it, though? Because despite "having it all," there had always been a restless sense of something missing.

Until she had fallen into an opportunity. Her friend Kylie had become engaged and was endlessly debating the perfect venue for the wedding.

Shelby happened to know someone with a villa in France. She'd put the two parties in touch and then, because she'd attended so many exclusive events, she had acted as an adviser on details like menu and decor and accommodations for the guests. It had been fun in a very different way than other things in her life had been fun. That restless sense of something missing had been held at bay for the entire time she'd been involved in Kylie's wedding.

The wedding had turned out so well that soon another friend had asked for Shelby's help with an event.

And so her company Eventually had been born. Despite the fact getting the first check for money she had actually earned had been more heady than the very expensive champagne served at Kylie's wedding, Shelby was aware her company was really nothing more than a fun little hobby. Still, that didn't stop her from thinking about it. A lot. When she wasn't dabbling in actual event planning, she was collecting a growing portfolio of perfect locations.

Each time she collected a picture and information on a new potential location, she would have a wonderful, dreamy sense of exactly the kind of event that belonged there.

And then, into her life had come a wicked stepmother. Though Shelby still hated to admit this, it might have been one of those blessings in disguise.

Lydia Barkley was not like the kind of women Shelby's father, Boswell, usually dated. His taste usually ran to women, admittedly like Shelby's own mother, who were coiffed, sophisticated, fit society women—or cleverly disguised wannabes.

No, Lydia was stout. Her brutally short hair sometimes looked as if she had cut it herself. She wore makeup badly. Shelby doubted she knew Prada from Gucci, though she owned both. She was blunt rather than subtle. Still, her father found her refreshing.

Lydia had a successful law practice. She *liked* working. From the outset, it had been apparent she viewed cosseted, pampered women with very thinly veiled contempt.

Which Shelby deduced meant Lydia held her died-too-young mother in contempt. You didn't really need an excuse to dislike your stepmother, but Shelby was glad to have one.

Not that it mattered, anyway. Shelby had been twenty-six when her father had married Lydia, well past the age where she needed a mommy. In fact, for the most part, she was able to avoid the newlyweds. If her father and Lydia let her know they were arriving at the location Shelby was at, she quickly vacated it.

Still, there was no avoiding the obligatory "family" gatherings. Which was how she'd had her deduction about Lydia's contempt for her mother confirmed.

Her father—or maybe Lydia—had selected the Chelsea house for Christmas. Shelby thought it was a poor choice. She found London drab in the winter. Her current boyfriend, Keith—the latest in a long string—had refused to come, so she had bought him a ticket for the Cayman Islands, where she planned to meet him at the Kane property as soon as it was humanly possible.

Coming down the stairs to join Lydia and Boswell, Shelby—dreading making excuses for Keith, whom she knew her father did not approve of—stopped dead in her tracks outside of the double doors of the parlor at the sound of her own name coming off Lydia's lips.

What she had heard changed Shelby's entire existence and cemented her dislike for her stepmother.

"Boswell, I'm concerned about Shelby."

Sure you are, Shelby thought. She waited for her father to protest discussing his daughter with an interloper, and a dowdy one at that, but no, all she heard was her father's mild "Oh?"

It was all the encouragement Lydia needed.

"She's obviously being used by Keith."

Her father, again, was given an opportunity not to indulge in this kind of backstabbing gossip, but he did not.

Instead, he said with a sigh, "Obviously."

Obviously? That hurt! The truth felt more complex. Shelby sometimes wondered if she wasn't using Keith.

He suited her. He filled the need for companionship without ever bringing up any sense she would have to commit to him.

Commitment could lead to other things.

Like children.

Shelby liked children. She liked them a lot. In fact, she got on famously with most of the children she knew.

Probably because, until Eventually at least, her maturity had matched theirs. She was pretty sure she'd make a terrible mother.

Still, aside from the qualification of being commitment-phobic, when was the last time Keith had paid for anything? Or even offered to pay for anything?

"In fact, Bosley—"

Ugh. How Shelby hated Lydia calling Boswell that horrible little endearment.

"I don't like the people she surrounds herself with. They're superficial, frivolous or users."

This was patently untrue! Wasn't it? Besides,

Shelby thought huffily, the people she hung around with wouldn't like Lydia, either.

Because of the way her step-mother wore her hair? Didn't that kind of prove Lydia's point?

"I've feared the same thing," her father said.

What?

"But Bosley, dear, it's really on you. You've overindulged poor Shelby to the point of ruination."

Poor Shelby? Ruination?

"I tried to make up for the fact she had no mother," Boswell said.

"Of course you did, dear. But, in fact, I fear she did have a mother, and I fear she will end up just like her if you don't sort it out."

Shelby felt a familiar shiver of dread at the mention of her mother, which she shrugged off in favor of indignation.

Here was her father's opportunity! To leap to her defense, and the defense of her mother! It wasn't as if it was her mother's fault she had died.

Or was it? a voice in Shelby's head insisted on whispering. There were still so many unanswered questions around her mother's death, a topic she had been shielded from since it had happened.

Willingly shielded from. Her father had protected her from the inevitable gossip that surrounded such a beautiful, young, well-known woman's demise, and Shelby was grateful for that.

Wasn't she?

Of course she was! She could have searched the details online at any time if she needed more information. The thought of looking up her mother made her feel sick to her stomach, as if she was spying or prying or being disloyal to her memories.

"I've had some thoughts," Lydia said. And then she had outlined, in quite great detail, what those thoughts were.

So, Shelby had been 100 percent prepared when, after an awkward Christmas dinner, her father had suggested a meeting and they had all moved to the stuffy library of the Chelsea house.

Lydia, Shelby noticed, was wearing her lawyer face.

But before Lydia could announce the plan Shelby had already overheard—that she would not receive an allowance, or have access to the family jet, or any of the residences around the world, or their lovely staff who cooked and cleaned and looked after her, or even a driver— Shelby made an announcement of her own.

"I've started a little business," she said casually. "It's doing quite well."

Okay, that was a bit of a stretch, but the look of skepticism on Lydia's face egged her on.

"I've decided that I'm perfectly capable of making it on my own."

Her father had looked flummoxed, and Lydia had looked put out at having her wicked-stepmother scheme snatched out from under her. Both their expressions had made Shelby's announcement well worth it!

And given her just the incentive she needed to show them by taking her business to the next level.

Now Shelby was eighteen months into Eventually.

Annoyingly, her father and Lydia—and her own niggling doubts—had been absolutely on point about Keith.

Starting her own business had brought out a surprisingly pragmatic side in her. Shopping for your own toilet paper could do that.

And, increasingly, she had seen that she had imbued Keith with poetic qualities of romance and charm, when in fact, he was lazy and lacked goals, focus and ambition. He did not pull his own weight or pay his own way, even when her funds dried up. Instead of offering to step up to the plate, he sulked.

She was not sure why she had set such a low bar for herself. She had fallen into a relationship apparently on a shared value of not wanting to get married and not wanting to have children. Recognizing this aversion to commitment, she swore off love with a sense of relief, rather than loss, and gave herself over to her business with her whole heart and soul.

Shelby had not so much left Keith as let him

fade from the picture, not as angry with him as she was with herself.

What had she been thinking?

She threw herself—gratefully—into surviving her new and shocking reality.

She was a young woman who had never fried an egg, driven a car, paid a bill. She had always been surrounded by luxury and now she lived in a cubbyhole about the same size as any of her closets around the world. It felt as if she had been thrown into a new country where she had no map and did not speak the language.

Still, she was shocked—and delighted—to discover a hidden truth about herself. Shelby Kane was a fighter!

She *liked* making it on her own. She *liked* conquering the challenges that she faced every day.

And, as extra incentive for success, she was determined to show her father and Lydia she was not going to be the ruined object of their pity!

CHAPTER TWO

THOUGH HER TALENTS might have been born of complete desperation, Shelby found she had a knack for business as she pushed Eventually to the next level.

Shelby's connections had helped her to survive and thrive. While walking a fine line—"I'm doing this for fun not because I have to"—her business was becoming the go-to among the rich and famous for the best birthday party or anniversary or family reunion or charity fundraiser.

She'd quickly established that her specialty—what set her apart from all the others—was venue. She knew people who owned some of the most spectacular real estate on earth, and she was able to use her name to talk them into sharing it for the right cause and the right price. Her father allowed her to use Kane properties if it was for her fledgling business, though, annoyingly, he seemed to find her business pursuits *cute* and she had the feeling he was just waiting for her to either fail spectacularly or lose interest.

But she wasn't losing interest. If anything, she felt more interested in life every single day. That portfolio of collected photos and locations that she saved for extra-special events kept getting thicker and thicker. When she approached people, even strangers, they were usually surprisingly amenable to her enthusiastic vision, and to having their property enjoyed by others. For the right price or even the right publicity.

And so Angela Fillmore's eighth birthday had been held at a 150-room castle in the Blue Ridge Mountains outside of Asheville, North Carolina.

Kate and Landon Whitley had hosted four hundred guests to help them celebrate fifty years of marriage on a private island in the Caribbean.

The Wellingtons had welcomed four generations of family for a reunion on board a super-yacht off the coast of Greece.

The Ladies Aid League of New York had held their charity ball—their most successful event ever—at a luxurious Martha's Vineyard estate.

The learning curve was steep. Sometimes, when the smoke had cleared, Shelby had not made as much money as she had hoped, and on one disastrous occasion she had even lost money, and the stress of planning events was often unrelenting.

She lay awake at night thinking of bills. And of juggling Peter to pay Paul. And going over all the hundreds of details involved in creating a successful event.

And yet, she was succeeding. She had been able to hire an assistant, Marcus. And underlying the hum of worry and stress was a sense of satisfaction. Accomplishment. The truth was, she was finding herself—her strength, her creativity, her confidence and even her leadership abilities—in the task of being responsible for people's hopes and happiness.

And then Lydia had thrown her a curveball. She wanted Shelby to plan her father's sixty-fifth birthday party.

Shelby was not sure if it was, on Lydia's part, a test or a fledgling act of trust.

What she did know was that she *needed* not just to take this on, but also to make it her most spectacular event ever. She needed them to see how far she had come, she needed to prove this wasn't just some cute little game she was playing that she would soon lose interest in and come back begging for their assistance.

Shelby had refused Lydia's money. And said she would be happy to give the party as a gift to her father.

And she had known exactly where to have it.

In that folder she kept, there was one place that stood above them all. She had come across it in a magazine in the waiting room of a corporate office whose CEO's anniversary she was planning. The magazine had been about ranching, of all things.

It had drifted open to a photo that had taken Shelby's breath away and made her heart sigh with longing, or maybe even knowing.

The magazine article had been about the history of ranching in that part of Southern Alberta. The photo that captured her soul had been of a huge timber-frame barn, with a traditional gambrel roof. It sat, solid, on the edge of a wooded ravine, the mountains beyond that.

The description said the 150-year-old structure was on the Mountain Waters Ranch and had been decommissioned as a barn for over fifty years. It was now used exclusively to service the surrounding ranch community, hosting graduations, weddings, family reunions, birthday parties and anniversaries.

She had looked at that photo as if it was a long, cool drink and she was dying of thirst. The photo was taken outside the huge, wide-open double doors that led into the barn. One might expect a barn to be dark, but surprisingly, light poured in from double doors, also open, at the other end of the structure. Those doors framed a painting-like vista of valleys and mountains.

The cavernous barn interior was both majestic and cozy with open beams and rafters. Again— surprisingly—gorgeous, gigantic chandeliers hung at the center of each of the four crossbeams.

The slatted wooden ceiling and the walls had aged to the color of maple syrup.

Though there were no people in the photo, it was obvious the space had been set up for a wedding. At least two hundred matching chairs, white, with pale blue bows on the back, faced those incredible open back doors and the views beyond them.

Shelby, of course, had recognized her own weakness because of the horrible Keith choice, and was totally sworn off romance.

It felt like way too close a call, a brush with disaster. What if, caught in the thrall of romantic illusion, she had actually married him? It made her shudder to think!

And yet, when she had seen that photo, it was as if every lesson she'd learned evaporated. It was as if some much-suppressed part of herself surged to the forefront. Shelby—who didn't even have a boyfriend, and hoped to never have one again—had had the completely ridiculous thought *This is where I will get married.*

Why would she need to get married? Running her business took all her time and energy and was fulfilling in ways she had not expected in the least. She was free of the *neediness* of women who pursued a relationship—and marriage—as if that was some kind of holy grail that would give them every single satisfaction they had ever sought in life.

Still, even knowing it was not rational—lying to herself that her interest was strictly professional—she had surreptitiously torn that picture from the magazine and folded it carefully into her handbag to put in her portfolio.

Since she knew—rationally—that she was not getting married, why not impress her father with this location for the most spectacular sixty-fifth birthday party ever?

That, however, was proving to be a major problem, because Samuel Waters, the reclusive widowed billionaire who owned the ranch, turned out not to be one of those amenable owners who could be persuaded to share a special place.

Even with all her sources, Shelby could not lay her hands on a phone number for him. She did find an email.

But Mr. Waters had only answered one of her three dozen emails. With a single word.

No.

Without having met him, Shelby was pretty sure she disliked Samuel Waters nearly as much as her wicked stepmother.

Which was not mature.

Really, she had hoped her perseverance over the many challenges of the past eighteen months would be worth something. She had hoped she would be much more grown-up by now than to dislike someone sight unseen.

Though, she hoped to be seeing Mr. Waters very

soon. She was not taking his *no* as a final answer. She was sure she could convince him. She was going to beard the lion in his own den.

Or on his own ranch as the case might be.

The range road, finally, began a gradual uphill climb. It wound through lovely copses of trees, the green of their leaves new and vibrant. Every now and then Shelby caught sight of a creek meandering beside the road.

She opened her window and sure enough, she could hear the babbling of the waters. And birdsong. The air had a purity and a crispness to it she was not sure she had ever experienced before. She suddenly did not feel the aloneness as a burden.

She came to the top of the hill and stopped. For the second time, Shelby got out of the car, taking in the incredible view of the valley below her.

The road wound down to a ranch and entered under a wooden archway with a wrought iron sign hanging from the thick log crossbeam. The sign had a single cowboy in relief, gazing off into the distance, and the words *Mountain Waters Ranch*.

From her viewpoint on the hill, the buildings looked as if they belonged to a child's toy set. It was obvious this was a very prosperous operation. There was a white barn, and some outbuildings, corrals, and a sandy riding arena. There was also a runway and an airplane hangar, which was good because she was not sure about asking people to drive this far for a party.

She was pretty certain the wicked stepmother could arrange for the Kane private jet to ferry people from the Calgary International Airport. And maybe Lydia could even pony up for some helicopter transport.

The view gently swept the preoccupation with logistics from Shelby's mind. In the distance, where fields gave way to a valley, was *the* barn, perched on the edge of a ravine carved out by thousands of years of water flowing through it.

The photos had not done it justice. The weathered building, hewn, weather-grayed logs with thick chinking between them, was huge and spectacular.

But at least as spectacular as that barn, situated at the center of the ranch, like a hub, was a sprawling log house that had not been in the photo Shelby had seen.

Several gigantic trees shaded the wraparound porch, but smoke chugged out of a river-rock chimney a defense against the mountain crispness in the air.

Shelby felt the oddest longing looking at the place.

Somehow, the house and the buildings fit here, as if they had been here forever and would stay here forever.

There was a solidness about the Mountain Waters Ranch that made her sigh with a deep and surprising sense of yearning. That cluster of buildings in that wide valley whispered of tradition and history and family. A place, isolated from the world, where people had found safety and sanctuary, and made *home* for a hundred years, or maybe longer.

Her feeling that it would be perfect for her father's sixty-fifth deepened to a conviction that it was the *only* place that would do.

And she discovered how invested she was in wanting to be the one to give him that extra-special day, to show him she loved him, despite his falling under the sway of her wicked stepmother. And that she was worthy, somehow...

She got back in the little car and drove the shaded road down the hill. The road curved left to the house and right to the barn and outbuildings. She took the left turn and found herself at a parking pad, in front of a neat yard. Again, she felt that sigh, almost like recognition.

A swing dangled from a branch of one of those trees. There was an expanse of well-tended lawn, vibrantly green. A bed of red tulips formed a half circle around the veranda, and the thick green leaves stirred in the breeze.

Wide stone steps made their way up to a deep veranda scattered with furniture, though Shelby's eyes rested on the two rocking chairs, side by side, which looked out across the sweeping yard and beyond to the buildings, and beyond that to the endless mountains.

A child's shout, high-pitched with excitement, drew her attention away from the house. She turned, shaded her eyes and saw *him*.

The man, probably fifty yards away, was the quintessential picture of a cowboy. Booted and hatted, he was leaning on his elbows on the top rail of a wooden pole fence that enclosed a riding arena. One long leg was hitched on the bottom rail. He had on a dark denim shirt, jeans faded to nearly white and, of course, the cowboy boots and the hat. There was something in his stature, the broadness of his shoulders, the leanness at his waist and hips, that suggested both power and grace.

He turned and gave her a cursory look, the brim of his white cowboy hat keeping his face shaded.

Even though she couldn't see his features, she could feel something stir in her.

Be still, my heart, she commanded herself. She thought he would come to her—how many strangers would show up here, after all?—but no, he turned his attention away from her, as if her appearance held no interest to him whatsoever.

Shelby felt *dismissed*, in the same way she had when she'd received that single-word response to her emails. It was a somewhat new feeling in her Kane world. She was also aware that, despite the rudeness of the email, she had expected a certain rural friendliness, a tipped hat, a *howdy, ma'am*.

She debated. Go knock on the door of the house? The tulips held some promise of hospitality, didn't they?

But then she spotted the source of that shout that had drawn her attention in the first place.

Oh, for heaven's sake. Of course the cowboy hadn't come over! He was supervising a child. A small, adorable child. She looked to be about five, and she was sitting on a chubby palomino pony on the other side of the fence from the man.

Shelby started to make her way toward the riding arena, but the heel of one shoe sank deep into the spring soft ground. She contemplated that for a moment. Shoes of this quality were not in the *budget* if she broke the heel.

She took both shoes off and went forward barefoot. Despite her control of the first impression going somewhat awry, Shelby reminded herself of her mission. She also reminded herself maturity was required.

The little girl suddenly saw Shelby. Her expression was anything but curious. The child looked furious!

As Shelby approached the rail at the far end of the arena, the little girl pulled the pony around, pointed him in Shelby's direction and laid her heels to him. He reluctantly broke into a trot, and then a clunky canter as she pummeled him with her legs.

She arrived at Shelby in a cloud of dust. As it

settled, Shelby took her in. Dark, wild curls tumbled out from under a pink cowboy hat. She had a leather-fringed vest on over a Pawsy-Poo T-shirt. The only reason Shelby knew who Pawsy-Poo was was because she had done a themed party for a little girl obsessed with the cartoon character.

The child had on a leather skirt that matched her vest, with black tights. The ensemble ended at her feet, which were encased in pink cowboy boots.

She had beautifully delicate features, eyes that reminded Shelby of the deer that she had encountered earlier. She had a tiny bow of a mouth, though her loveliness was distorted by her scowl and the downturn of said bow.

Peripherally, she was aware of the cowhand now striding along the arena toward them.

"Hel—"

She was given no opportunity to finish her greeting.

The child pulled a toy from a holder at her waist and pointed it directly at Shelby.

"Bang."

If Shelby was not mistaken, she had just been shot with a fashion doll.

She had no choice. She dropped her shoes, staggered backward and clasped her chest. She closed her eyes, let her knees fold under her and fell to the ground with as much drama as possible.

"I've been shot," she whispered, hoping the

grass was not staining her outfit, because like the shoes, she did not have the means to replace it.

When she heard a reluctant giggle, Shelby quit worrying about the outfit, or about being mature. Maturity was not all it was cracked up to be, anyway.

CHAPTER THREE

SHELBY LAY THERE, STILL, until she felt a shadow fall over her. She opened her eyes. Then she felt as if she really had been shot.

The man gazing down at her, from underneath the wide brim of that cowboy hat, was 100 percent gorgeous. And he emitted a kind of power and confidence that whispered a warning to Shelby: *Not just a cowboy.*

His eyes, identical to the child's, were one shade darker than the most decadent of dark chocolates, and fringed with an abundance of lashes that Epais would have killed to be able to use for an advertisement.

His hair was off his face, held back by the cowboy hat, but it escaped out over his ears and brushed his neck, with a promise of dark curls just like the child's. His hair was too long, and yet the look was undeniably sexy.

He had high cheekbones, a straight, strong nose, full lips and a hint of a cleft in his chin.

He gazed at her for a moment, and his eyes narrowed, as if he was debating what to do. He was obviously not amused by her reaction to being downed by the doll.

There was definite reluctance when, after a moment, he held out his hand to her. Which was still a long way from *howdy, ma'am*.

A feeling engulfed her, like a premonition. Not that Shelby had ever been given to such things.

If she took his hand, her life would be changed forever. In ways she could not control. Shelby Kane liked control, a lot.

What she did not like was powerlessness.

And yet that was what she felt as she reached out to his proffered hand. Powerless. As if she had given in to a spell, one loaded with a kind of savage sizzle rather than sweet enchantment.

The sizzle was confirmed as his hand closed around hers with pure and breathtaking masculine strength.

Shelby had never experienced a touch that was quite that real or that raw before. As she was yanked unceremoniously to her feet, his easy strength made some awareness—primal—tingle up and down her spine.

For a moment, she was sure he felt it, too, as she saw a flash of startled awareness in his eyes. But then he let go of her hand abruptly and scowled.

Unfortunately, his stern look was extraordinarily sexy, especially because of its contrast to those untamed curls.

"Hannah," he snapped, looking away from her and to the little girl, who still sat on her pony, "it's not polite to shoot at the guests."

"You can't shoot someone with a doll," Hannah pointed out. She wagged the doll at him—it was wearing an outfit not unlike her own, minus the hat—and tucked it back in her waistband.

Shelby caught a look on the man's face. Vulnerable. Unable to counter the inarguable logic of a small child. For a man who looked as if the whole world belonged to him, as if there was no situation he would not bring indomitable confidence to, he seemed to be in over his head.

"Besides, I don't like her," Hannah announced.

"You're shattering my myths about farm friendliness," Shelby said, smiling at her.

"It's not a farm," the child said, not charmed. "It's a ranch."

"You're being very rude," the man said.

A puffy lip stuck out in an unrepentant pout.

The man presented Shelby with his hand. For the second time.

"Sam Waters," he said.

This was Sam Waters? It confirmed her initial intuition that he was more than a cowboy. It occurred to Shelby her allergy to internet sleuthing had not stood her well this time.

Had she known he was not old and stodgy, she could have been better prepared.

Though gazing at him, she was not quite sure how you prepared for *this*.

"Shelby Kane," she said, taking his hand. She should have been ready this time. But she wasn't. His grasp was mind-blowingly strong, warm, sexy. And brief.

"This is my daughter, Hannah."

Hannah glowered at her.

"Say hello to Miss Kane," Sam said sternly, "and then apologize for assaulting her with your doll and telling her you don't like her. You don't even know her."

"Hello, Miss Kane. I'm sorry I don't like you."

Shelby giggled at how Hannah had circumvented the apology, which earned her a dark look from the very sexy daddy.

"I wasn't expecting you. The agency told me they weren't going to send anyone else," he said, taking off his hat and running a hand through glossy hair. Loose curls sprang up under his touch.

That hair! Unfairly gorgeous.

What agency?

"I don't need a nanny!"

Sam regarded his daughter for a moment, then slammed his hat back onto his head.

They thought Shelby was a nanny!

"Of course you don't," Shelby said, earning her a look of reluctant interest from the child and a glance of grave annoyance from the man.

That wasn't exactly *I am not a nanny.*

"You're a city girl, aren't you?" Sam asked. His voice had a gravelly tone to it that felt as if it was scraping across her skin. And not in an unpleasant way.

Best not to let him know that!

"I prefer to think of myself as a woman," Shelby said.

Especially around him. She thought about how she had earlier contemplated the phrase *boyfriend.*

He would never be anyone's boyfriend.

And she didn't want to be seen as a girl around him.

Something extraordinarily adult was swirling in the air between them. It was a good thing Shelby was now 100 percent a career woman!

Sam Waters cocked his head at her.

"Woman," he said, his tone flat. "Noted."

That was not *exactly* how she wanted him to notice her. Still, they were getting off on the wrong track.

"I'm from New York," she said.

He nodded, as if this was not entirely unexpected, and not a good thing, either. He rocked back on his heels and looked into the distance.

"I guess that's why they're called International Nanny Services. Though I'm surprised *nanny* is still a politically acceptable term."

There was lots of sarcastic emphasis on *politi-*

cally acceptable—clearly a dig at her correcting him about being a girl. Shelby realized that she had to tread very carefully at the moment.

For some reason the lines were blurring. It actually felt as if she *had* arrived here as a nanny, not looking to him to provide his ranch for a sixty-fifth birthday party. She allowed herself to glance off toward that timber-frame barn.

Though the barn would be absolutely perfect.

"You know, if you're going to bring your city sensibilities here with you, you can just get back in—" he leveled a look at her vehicle "—that toy car and go back where you came from."

"It looks like a car a clown drives at the circus," Hannah chimed in.

"Hence the agency being reluctant to send people," Shelby said to the pair of them, diplomacy be damned.

He looked at her narrowly. It occurred to her he was not a man accustomed to being challenged.

Given what she wanted from him, couldn't she, just this once, have held her tongue?

She had to tell him the truth and she had to tell him right now. On the other hand, Sam Waters did not look as if he was going to be amenable to giving over his ranch for a party.

What if he knew her better? What if she knew him better?

She was kidding herself. Somehow this wasn't even about the party anymore. Shelby didn't just want to see inside that house, it felt as if she *needed* that. To set foot in a place where stockings had hung on the same mantel for a hundred years or more, where people had sat on those porch rockers, maybe holding hands…

Sam sighed. "Can I assume you don't ride?"

"You can. I don't actually like horses."

She was treated to identical aghast expressions from the father and daughter duo. She looked at the pony.

"Toy horses excepted, of course."

She watched a reluctant smile twitch at Sam's lips.

"I don't need a nanny," Hannah said again. "Buckie is fine! I love him. He takes care of me."

"The pony?" Shelby asked. A pony was looking after the child?

"No, that's Rascal," Sam said. "Buckie is the ranch cook."

"Buckie?"

"Nicknames tend to go hand in hand with ranch work. He does childcare in a pinch, but it's not ideal. We're pretty much a society of men out here. She needs a woman."

"I don't!" Hannah cried. "You can't be my mommy. My mommy died."

For a moment, the angry mask slipped, and all Shelby saw in the little girl was immense and bottomless pain.

"My mommy died, too," she said quietly.

The connection between them was brief and intense. Suddenly she knew this little girl *needed* her.

It was shocking to realize that in her twenty-eight years on the planet, she had never, ever felt that before.

Needed.

She wondered, briefly, why she had such an aversion to having children when, really, who needed you more than them?

She felt a sudden, totally unwanted tickle down her spine. She could suddenly remember herself, at about the age of this child, *needing* with a terrible desperation.

It wasn't quite a memory. The realization was followed by that familiar feeling of blankness that she always had about her early childhood.

She shook it off, and watched as Hannah whirled the fat pony around and took off down the arena, stirring up clouds of dust behind her.

Shelby glanced at Sam's face as his daughter rode away.

Maybe because some secret of her own had threatened to surface, she saw his with stunning clarity. He was a man who obviously had complete control of an empire. When she had searched for his contact info, she had found out his business portfolio and holdings were immense. They easily rivaled her father's.

But all his billions and all his power had not been able to save his daughter from sorrow.

As a daddy on his own, it seemed possible he was in way over his head.

Maybe, for once in her life, Shelby could put the needs of others ahead of her own. Such a noble sentiment made going along with a little white lie—committing the sin of omission— okay, didn't it?

No, it did not.

She drew in a breath. The woman she had been eighteen months ago would have gone along with the mistaken-identity thing, played it out for a bit.

But she couldn't. It wouldn't further her cause in the end, anyway.

Or maybe it was something about him, about Sam Waters, that made anything short of 100 percent integrity seem as if it was not acceptable.

"Look, I'm not—"

A sound stopped her midsentence. A man was thundering directly toward them on a horse. She could not be certain he was in complete control. Was the horse running away? Stampeding? Were they about to be crushed?

Shelby thought about jumping over the nearby fence to avoid a collision, but she felt oddly protected by Sam, who made no evasive move as the horse came closer, standing his ground, calm and strong.

Just when it seemed as if the horse was going

to crash right into them—she slid behind Sam, though he did not even flinch—the horse slammed to a halt, practically sitting down on his back legs the stop was so abrupt.

"Boss," the lean cowboy on the horse said. "There's been an accident at the round pen. I think we might need to chopper Jim out of here."

Sam's stillness was gone. He was already running.

He turned back. "Have you got this?"

Shelby nodded. Of course she had it. What other option was there?

Sam called Hannah from the hospital to make sure she was okay and to tell her good night.

He thought his daughter would be beside herself at his sudden departure and being handed over to the brand-new nanny, but her first question was for Jimmy. It was a small thing, but her ability to be concerned about others gave him hope that, in the sea of single-parenting confusion, maybe he was managing to get the odd thing right.

"Is he okay?" Hannah asked with touching and genuine concern.

"Yes, he's fine. He broke his arm."

"Does he have a cast?" she asked, not *when will you be home*, not *I hate the new nanny*.

"Yes, he does."

"Can I draw on it?"

The mystery of his daughter: How did she know people drew on casts? She had probably seen it on television.

Did he let her watch too much TV? So convenient, sometimes...

Would the woman who'd appeared in their lives so unexpectedly know things like that?

"How's, uh, Miss Kane?"

"She said I can call her Shelby. I like her."

"You do?" He tried to strip his genuine astonishment from his voice.

"Yes. She's nice."

"She is?"

"She's not really a nanny. She's just going to be my friend."

CHAPTER FOUR

CLEVER, SAM THOUGHT, for Shelby Kane to recognize his daughter's aversion to nannies and skirt around it.

He allowed himself to feel marginally hopeful that this time it was going to work out, even while he experienced a shiver of discomfort.

Miss Kane, in their very brief acquaintance, had made him feel something.

He didn't like it when he realized what that feeling was. Some awareness of her as a woman had shivered along his spine, even before he had taken her hand. Since the death of his wife, he knew all about the painfulness of firsts: birthdays celebrated without her, Christmas. You could sort of brace yourself for the swamp of feelings if the event was on a calendar.

But this first had taken him entirely by surprise, like a hit up the side of the head: finding a woman attractive.

For a man who had lost way too much to love,

Sam recognized that shiver he had felt for what it was: a warning.

It was flashing brightly in his brain like a neon sign: *Danger. Stay back.*

He'd traveled the treacherous path of love and loss a few too many times now. Only a fool would embark on that journey again.

It was dark by the time he landed the helicopter back at the ranch and helped a drowsy Jimmy to the bunkhouse.

"Take it easy for a few days," he told the hand.

"I hate leaving you shorthanded at this time of year."

"You know ranches," Sam said, even though he hated being shorthanded, too. The ranch was the least of his many business obligations, but it always seemed to be jostling for more time than he had to give it.

Still, he had every hope the new nanny might make his schedule a little more manageable.

"Sorry, boss."

There was injured pride in that statement. No cowboy wanted a hospital visit after getting tossed from a green colt.

"Hey, stuff happens." Only Sam didn't say *stuff*. He said a word he couldn't say when he was wearing his daddy hat and that he was pretty sure the nanny would not approve of.

He walked back through the darkness to the house. He stopped before he arrived. Someone was sitting on the front porch in one of the rocking chairs, wrapped in a blanket against the chill of the mountain spring evening.

It was the new nanny.

He felt a shiver of doubt. Should he call her Shelby? Or Miss Kane? He was annoyed at the uncertainty. He made decisions where millions of dollars were on the line with less thought than this.

He knew, from that jolting awareness of her, that the uncertainty ran deeper than what to call her, so he hesitated in the darkness awhile longer, studying her.

Sam remembered how her hand had felt in his when he had lifted her off the ground. Some dangerous current had passed between them, and he had seen awareness of it pass through her eyes, too.

But that was probably a natural reaction. He had not touched a woman since Beth had died. Such impulses could be controlled.

It was the other thing that seemed more dangerous. Sam remembered how she had looked at him a little too intently, as if she saw something he did not want her to see.

As if his every uncomfortable uncertainty was on full display. Especially when it came to raising his little girl on his own.

Every day, he tried to find balance between his business and his parenting obligations.

Business was easier, cut-and-dried.

Parenting, not so much. He walked in the unfamiliar land of not having answers. How much television was too much? Was it okay to let Hannah play the occasional game on his phone? What was he supposed to do with all that hair? Should she be picking her own outfits?

And bigger questions. The ranch was as close to happy as either of them had gotten since Beth had died. But was it okay to raise her here? Didn't she need *more*? More friends her own age, more things to prepare her for school?

School. Next year. He had to make decisions. He was good at decisions. Usually.

Now they nagged him. Did Hannah need more women? Even though Hannah had reacted violently to the suggestion, didn't she need some of that softness around her, that feminine energy that was in pretty short supply at the ranch?

Feminine energy. Shelby Kane had that in spades, even with her slender figure hidden in the folds of a blanket.

She was way too pretty for this job. Sam didn't like that he had noticed, especially her eyes. He might have initially said her eyes were brown, but that wasn't true. Up close, he had seen they were so shot through with flecks of gold and green that he wasn't quite sure what color they were.

Her hair was loose and thick. Earlier in the

day, the spring sun shining on it reminded him of honey in a jar. And her mouth...

He wished the agency would have sent a nanny like that one on television. The one who looked like a refrigerator in a pantsuit.

Shelby represented a complication of the variety he didn't need. When he'd helped her up off the ground, he'd felt that *complication* jolt through him.

Still, Hannah had actually said she liked her.

Had they connected because Shelby—he had decided to call her that, instead of Miss Kane—knew what it was to be a little girl drowning in sorrow?

That gave him a hope that maybe they could make this work.

Because when he'd first seen her, out of the corner of his eye, when she had walked up to the arena, he'd seen her get that heel stuck in the ground. The footwear choice alone signaled she didn't have the slightest idea what she was getting into.

When he'd observed her up close, he had recognized the name inside those shoes. Once, he'd been a part of that world.

Like generations before him, Sam had been born and raised on this ranch. But unlike those who came before him, and to his family's distress, he'd wanted a bigger world.

In university he'd been pulled toward technology, a field as far removed from the gritty realities of cows and land and weather and hard, physically demanding work as a man could get.

And yet, he was well aware, it was the combination of the worlds that had allowed Sam his rocket ride to success. His upbringing had given him drive and toughness, a relentless work ethic, an ability to think on his feet and handle challenges. He'd chased success and found it beyond his wildest dreams.

For a blink in time, he'd been the man with success and money and power beyond imagining.

And then he'd found love. In a way, Beth had been like him. She came from hardworking roots, but she had found fame in the culinary world, and by the time he'd met her, she was a celebrity with her own restaurants, cookbooks, internet channels and television specials.

For a blink in time, they had been the "it" couple. They had graced the covers of magazines and conquered the world. From the outside and from the inside, they had been the couple with everything.

Though Sam had redefined *everything* when he had held his baby daughter in his arms for the first time. The ranch—family—suddenly called him. He liked spending time there. He and Beth loved bringing Hannah to Mountain Waters for weekends, longer stays in the summer, at Christmas. Hannah had ridden with her grandfather, tucked into the front of his saddle, since she was a baby.

And then, Sam Waters's time in the sun had been over.

His father had gotten sick and died. His mother, her heart broken, followed with stunning swiftness.

Still reeling from those losses, Sam listened as Beth told him she wasn't feeling well. He knew, right away, that she had been trying to protect him because of his other heartbreaks. Had that delay mattered? If she had told him sooner—if he had *noticed*—could the outcome have been changed?

The diagnosis was devastating, as was the illness.

And then Sam, who only a moment ago had every single thing a man could ever dream of, was alone in the world, save for a small child who was trusting him not to break under the weight of all his shattered dreams.

Sam was left with the crushing knowledge that a man's sense that he was powerful was a complete illusion. When it counted, he was not.

And he was also left a single dad, in a world that wanted to feed on his grief and vulnerability.

Suddenly, the ranch he'd left behind—the life he'd left behind—offered sanctuary. He figured out how to run his other businesses from there.

Technology—and access to an airstrip—made it possible.

This was the place where his daughter was happy and protected from the public eye. This was the place where he could occasionally lose himself in the kind of hard, physical work that was a balm for the unrelenting pain, his awareness of his own powerlessness.

He was shocked how just seeing a woman on the porch had triggered all these thoughts. He hesitated, then went up the steps through the darkness.

Was that warning sign *Danger* flashing a little less brightly?

"Miss Kane," he said out loud.

"Shelby," she said.

He was aware he had been hoping for that, and that it felt like a weakness to harbor such a hope.

"Sam," he responded, even though the familiarity took a board out of the high fence he needed to keep up between them.

Employer, employee, he told himself sternly. "How did things go with Hannah tonight?"

"She wouldn't take a bath, or let me touch her hair, but other than that, good."

"Her hair," he said. "It's a good thing I know how to wrestle calves, because once a week I have to pin her down and get the tangles out of it."

He didn't admit how many times he had thought

of cutting Hannah's wild hair short. He hadn't because it would feel like a failure of sorts.

"You wrestle calves?" she asked. "Is that as exciting as it sounds?"

He did not want her to find anything about him *exciting*.

"It's hard and it's dirty. There's nothing romantic about it."

He wished he had not used that particular word. "Anyway, I said I know how. I'm not very hands-on with the ranch these days. I have a foreman who looks after the day-to-day operations. I'm pretty much an office guy now. And dad with hair challenges."

"Her room is a delight, by the way," Shelby said. He wondered if she wasn't trying to let him know that, despite the hair failure, he was doing something right. "I like the little tent in the corner. We sat in it to read a storybook."

He slid Shelby a glance. He was relieved things had gone well. It probably said way too much about his parenting that he wondered what contortions she'd had to do to squeeze into that tent.

"How's the injured man? Jim?"

It warmed him in a way that he didn't want to be warmed that there was such genuine concern in her voice for a stranger, a man she had never met. And that she'd remembered his name.

"I brought him back with me. He'll be okay. Broken arm. He'll be laid up for a bit."

"What happened to him?"

"He was riding a green colt. Things went sideways. It's a ranch. Stuff happens." This time he did say *stuff*. "What are you doing out here?" he asked.

She gazed up at him with those luminous eyes, which, in the moonlight, looked more green than gold or brown.

He'd rather she wasn't pretty, because that was just a complication on a ranch full of men. It was the same as putting a mare in with the herd. Pretty soon all those old reliable guys were acting silly and vying for attention.

The hands would probably all be picking the tulips and bringing her bouquets within a week.

Who was he kidding? It wasn't the hands he was worried about.

It was himself.

And it was the first time he'd had such a thought since Beth died. Shelby was bringing firsts he hadn't expected, and he didn't like it. It made him feel faintly resentful, as if she was intruding in a sacred place.

He needed to turn the wattage back up on that *Danger* sign.

"Didn't Buckie show you where to put your things?"

"Yes, that lovely room above the garage. It's very nice," she said.

"It's set up for you to cook for yourself if you

want to. But the nearest grocery store is a long way away. Buckie does all the cooking until you're set up, or if you'd rather not."

"Alvin's adorable, by the way."

"Alvin?"

"Oh, that's his real name."

Sam contemplated that. The ranch cook had been on the Mountain Waters Ranch long before he had. He'd been part of raising him. Of course, he knew his name was Alvin, because he signed the checks. But he'd never heard him called that before, ever.

The cook was a man whose idea of knowing the alphabet was having a swear word to match every letter.

Every single letter.

He wondered what the new nanny would think of *that*.

Adorable, he was not. Of course, Buckie, like every other guy in the place, would probably be on his best behaviour.

"It's so beautiful out here," she breathed, answering his question about what she was doing outside. "I wanted to just enjoy it for a bit."

Don't sit down with her.

But suddenly he felt exhausted, the day catching up with him. He took the rocker next to her. Why wouldn't he sit down with his daughter's new nanny? Wasn't it part of his parental responsibility? To get to know Shelby Kane?

But he knew that wasn't exactly why he'd taken the seat. And it couldn't totally be blamed on exhaustion, either. It was the look on her face.

Wonder. It pulled at some place in him that had not felt that for a long, long time. He should have heeded it as the danger level increasing, but he was too tired.

"I don't think I've ever seen stars like this," Shelby said.

He looked out at the star-encrusted night. He was astounded by the beauty of it, as if he'd been blind and suddenly could see. How long had it been since he'd had a moment like this? When he just felt so aware?

"And the sounds," she pointed out. "I thought it would be quiet in the country, but it's not."

Sure enough, he heard the cry of an owl, the deep lowing of faraway cattle, crickets chirping, a chorus of frogs down by the creek.

"I smell something, too," she said. "It's so pure. Like opening a bottle of champagne and the bubbles tickling your nose."

He noticed a scent as well, but it had nothing to do with the fresh fragrances of mountain air, pine, the clean breeze coming down off the snow-capped mountains, cattle.

It was her. The fact it was so subtle—not perfume or soap—made it shockingly sensual. He could not pinpoint it, but it was like a combination of flowers and spice and feminine mystery.

Sam felt—despite the fact he was trying to heed all the danger signs—for the first time in a long, long time, fully alive. He did not like it!

It occurred to him he had a professional duty here that he was neglecting. He should be finding out about her.

There was a little more to entrusting a person with your daughter's care than your daughter's endorsement.

She's nice.

Tempting to think that was enough, but it wasn't.

"I'm sorry I wasn't expecting you," he told her. "I haven't checked my personal email for a couple of days."

"That must be wonderful," she said wistfully.

Yeah, she'll see about that when a late spring storm comes through and knocks out all the power for a week or so.

She was, of course, completely unsuitable for this position, even if she did read storybooks in a tent.

CHAPTER FIVE

SHELBY KANE. By her own admission she was a city girl.

But, so far, every one of the nannies Sam had tried out had been completely incompatible with the job. Sometimes they had been run off by his daughter before he even had a chance to see how unsuitable they were.

Certainly Hannah had never once said, of any of them, *I like her*.

Besides, unsuitable or not, he had several business trips coming up, and now he was down a hand. If Shelby could get him through the remaining days of spring calving, that was all he could ask.

"You must like children a lot to become a nanny," he said, trying to feel his way into what he supposed was an interview of sorts. "I'm surprised you don't have your own. A family of your own who will miss you when you take these assignments."

A husband had not occurred to him, until right this second. He slid a look at her ring finger.

Bare.

What about a boyfriend, waiting in the wings? He told himself the only reason he would care about her personal life, at all, was because of any effect it might have on her duties.

"I've never wanted children," she said softly.

He frowned. That was an odd comment from someone who made her living tending children.

She hesitated for a moment. "I wasn't just enjoying the evening. I was waiting for you, actually."

It was a small statement, and yet it made him *feel* something. Again. Having developed quite a skill for avoiding pesky emotions, he didn't like this. And especially when he pinpointed the pang as longing. To come home and have a woman waiting for him.

Danger.

Again, she was the nanny. Professionalism. Employer, employee. He barely knew her. He was just tired. His defenses—which were considerable— were down a bit. Because defenses, like the endless miles of fences on a ranch, needed constant vigilance, repair, maintenance.

"I didn't put anything in the room Alvin showed me."

She hadn't settled in. What did that mean? A new record for leaving? She'd already figured out it was way too isolated up here?

"I have to tell you something," she said, her voice low, as if she was about to make a confession.

Her gallows tone made Sam brace himself for a multitude of possibilities.

I'm pregnant. I've already decided I'm not staying. Can my boyfriend come? Can I have the weekend off? Where's the mall?

"I'm not a nanny."

After telling him that simple truth, Shelby watched Sam Waters's face carefully.

He had removed his hat and was twirling it between long fingers. He really was unfairly gorgeous, with those loops of too-long curls framing his face. Here, sitting on the front porch, with his features illuminated by moonlight, his rugged good looks were even more obvious than they had been at their initial encounter.

She noticed his lashes again. The luscious darkness of his eyes. The masculine, symmetrical cut of strong, perfect features. The firmness of his lips, the faint puffiness of the lower one.

The stubble beginning to darken his cheeks and his chin accentuated his masculinity and made him look faintly roguish and entirely sexy.

She had talked about the scent on the air, but in truth she had noticed that before he sat down.

After, her senses had been engulfed by *him*, and the unexpected intimacy of the moment. She had been super aware of his nearness, his distinctive aroma, the hard line of muscle on his forearm as he rested it on the arm of the rocker. Despite the chill in the air, Sam was still in the same dark blue denim shirt—no jacket—and yet he seemed in no way cold, which made her even more aware of the robust appeal of the man.

He laughed at her announcement.

She liked the upward quirk of those firm lips, and the light that danced in the darkness of his eyes. She *really* liked his laughter. It was warm and engaging. It made her aware Sam Waters carried a weight, and that the laughter, however briefly, lifted it.

He actually looked relieved by her announcement, as if he'd been expecting something else.

"That's what Hannah said when I called from the hospital to tell her good night."

Something in Shelby's heart just melted. She must have already left the little girl when he'd called. There was a sweetness to his calling his child to say good night that a person wouldn't expect from the stern lines in his face.

That shadow of something like memory passed over her again. *A little girl waiting for a call that did not come.*

"Hannah told me that you're not a nanny. Given her aversion to them, I congratulate you on being so clever."

There. She could leave it at that. She had done

her due diligence. She could take false credit for him thinking she was clever.

Maybe she could spend a few days here, before she revealed the truth. Mountain Waters Ranch was doing something to her heart that made her not want to let go of it right away.

When Alvin had shown her around the house, she was not sure she had ever been in a place that felt so like *home*, despite the fact it was large and utterly magnificent. The kitchen was state-of-the-art. She had glimpsed a theater room.

It had been exquisitely renovated, with no expense spared, and yet, while having every modern amenity, it had remained true to its traditional roots.

Shelby had recognized the quality and timelessness of many of the furnishings and decorations. Like the Kane properties, this house held gorgeous, tasteful antiques, priceless rugs, rare paintings, authentic collectibles from many cultures.

But the polished golden log walls, the paned windows and the heartwood pine floors gave it a feeling of hominess that none of the interior designers of her father's many houses had ever achieved.

There was a sense here—worn into the floors and radiating from the magnificent log walls of that ranch house—of stability, of generations of gatherings around that harvest table in the dining room for special occasions, but ordinary ones, too.

The house had the layers of charm that came only when people actually called a place home. There were toys on the floor and a jigsaw puzzle, partially built, on the kitchen island. There was a calendar hanging with the boxes crowded with markings in a strong hand. Vet coming, dentist appointment, a birthday party—all the daily details of lives where people actually stayed and lived in one place.

In the living room there was a book, opened and face down, abandoned on the coffee table, and a sock peeked out from under an old, comfy-looking easy chair. A teddy bear with only one ear and the thread for his mouth half removed was flopped over on a sofa.

The focus of the room was a floor-to-ceiling river rock fireplace, the inner firebox burned black and with remnants of charcoal and ash in it. On the chunky wooden mantel, Shelby could clearly see the nails where socks were hung at Christmastime.

Alvin appeared to be the only staff member. It was more than obvious there were no servants discreetly in the background, slipping around returning everything to perfection as quickly as possible.

Her glimpse into the real lives of the Waterses had filled Shelby with a longing. To know more.

Or maybe deeper, and certainly more frightening, to fit. To belong.

Something tickled up her spine. Fear. Of wanting things she had decided, many years ago, that she could not have.

It would be almost a relief to get sent packing before those hidden desires got out of control. But her experience told her that to long for a sense of family was to set herself up for disappointment.

"I'm *really* not a nanny. I wasn't sent here by International Nanny Services."

Sam's frown deepened. He looked hard at her through narrowed gaze. His eyes, which had seemed the color of chocolate in the light of day, looked nearly black in the stripped-down light of the moon.

The laughter was completely gone from his expression.

"Who are you, then?" There was no friendliness in the question. That moment of connection between them was erased.

Completely.

She took a deep breath. "I *am* Shelby Kane. I'm just *not* a nanny."

"Then what are you doing here? Mountain Waters is not exactly on the beaten path. People don't arrive here by accident."

She took another deep breath. "I can see why you would assume I might be a nanny, then."

"I don't recall you correcting that assumption."

"I was in the middle of telling you who I really was when we were interrupted."

He was silent, and expressionless, but a muscle jumped intimidatingly in his jaw.

Shelby took a deep breath. "In my defense, I thought we were about to be trampled."

If she thought his look might soften a bit with sympathy, she had been mistaken.

"I actually run a company called Eventually," she said in a rush. "I contacted you, by email, about hosting an event at the timber-frame barn?"

His frown deepened. "I left my daughter with you," he growled. "Thinking you had qualifications."

It was as if he hadn't even heard the part about the event.

"Yes," she said, keeping her tone agreeable, "There was a misunderstanding."

"You could be *anybody*," he said, his tone low and dangerous.

"Well, yes, that's true, but—"

"Who are you?" he interrupted, and then he said a swear word. "I trusted you. Because the agency does thorough background checks. Their nannies are trained to look after small children."

For a moment, she felt her own ire rising. "Are you suggesting that I might be some sort of unsavory character, derelict in my duties to your daughter through lack of formal training? If you're that uncertain about me, maybe you better go check and make sure Hannah is safely asleep in her bed. With no signs of neglect."

Sam didn't move, but his expression didn't soften, either.

"I *helped* you," she pointed out, miffed.

"You lied to me."

"I did not," she sputtered.

Suddenly, below his anger, she saw his underlying insecurity about being a good parent. A wisp of wistfulness flitted through her mind. Had anyone ever held themselves to this fire for her?

"You didn't fail in the parenting department because there was a misunderstanding about my credentials," she said quietly.

"I didn't?" he snapped back, not soothed. "You could be a reporter from one of those despicable rags that feed on human misery, while *pretending* compassion."

At least he didn't see her as a potential kidnapper.

"I hope that hasn't happened to you."

His glare spoke volumes.

"You could," he continued, "have been one of those women who has decided my daughter needs a mother and I need a companion, and coincidentally, they'll be set for life if they snag me."

She didn't have to ask this time if that had happened. It was written in every cynical line of his face.

"I'm sorry. I'm familiar with the hazards of wealth and fame."

He cocked his head at her.

"I'm Boswell Kane's daughter."

There. That should reassure him that a gold digger hadn't tracked him down and inserted herself into his life. "I told you. I'm just here because I want to rent the timber-frame barn."

For a moment, he looked only puzzled. And then understanding dawned on his face.

"Now I recognize your name. You've sent me about thirty thousand emails."

"Three thousand, at the most," she came back with.

He did not look amused.

"And if you would have answered them," Shelby continued, "I wouldn't be here."

"I did answer. And you're still here."

It was pretty hard to argue with that.

"It just wasn't the answer you wanted, was it?" he asked, his tone cold.

Somehow, the way he said that made her feel like the spoiled girl she had once been, unable to take no for an answer, unable to believe she could not get her own way.

"And if I had answered the way you wanted, if I'd said yes, you can rent the barn for your event, you would still be here, wouldn't you? Taking measurements, and making plans, and disrupting the quiet and the routines of this place with constant air traffic, and shipments of stuff and staff coming, and finally people arriving for the *event*."

He managed to load that word with contempt, as if she had suggested a three-ring circus, or a carnival complete with a sideshow.

"How would they arrive?" Sam went on softly, and held up his hand when she went to reply. "No, no, let me guess. Private jets and helicopters and maybe a Mercedes-Benz bus or two. And then people traipsing all over the place, breaking off their heels in soft dirt—"

That landed! Shelby felt herself wince.

"And getting lost," he continued, "and spooking the livestock, and distracting the hands, threatening to sue me."

"I've done many large events on private properties as nice as this one," she said stiffly.

"Good! Get one of them."

"I'm a professional," she went on, with pride. "I know how to troubleshoot, and I also know it's a privilege to use a property like this. I would never abuse that privilege. I can provide references."

"That won't be necessary. Because I don't rent out the barn."

"Yes, you do," she said.

"How about if you don't call me a liar?"

"You called me one! I saw a photo of an event there."

"Look, I don't want to spar with you. I don't *rent*

out the barn. I make it available to friends and neighbors for the *right* occasion."

"The right occasion," she repeated. "Such as?"

"Sometimes a private function like an anniversary, or a wedding, but usually community events. The high school graduation ceremony and dance will be here in a little over a week."

"You don't even know what my occasion is."

"I don't know you. I don't care what your event is."

"What's the difference?" she demanded. "The disruption to your precious routines would be just the same."

"The difference is that these are the people who have stood with our ranch in good times and in bad. The difference is these are the people we've grown up with and grown old with. The difference is that I would know the first names of almost every single person who set foot on the place. The difference is we share the history of this valley."

There was that longing again, dangerous, and so appealing, as many dangerous things were.

A yearning for what she had never had.

Community. But she would not let him see how he had stung her. She would not beg!

CHAPTER SIX

SAM REALLY COULD not remember the last time he'd felt so angry with a person.

How dare Shelby Kane just waltz up here to his ranch thinking she could charm him into changing his mind? Impersonating a nanny?

"The difference is," he finished softly, "that I don't let people use this barn to make money. It's to give joy."

"You know," Shelby said with her chin titled and her tone haughty, as was befitting of the daughter of one of the world's richest men, "in our short acquaintance, I would say that is a topic you seem to know nothing about."

That stung! Not that he would ever let her see that she had landed an arrow.

There was more than a grain of truth in it. He had known joy, once. It had gone hand in hand with love. He was terrified of both now. Because once you had known them, the loss was shattering in every way it was possible to be shattered.

"And just for your information," Shelby said, "I

didn't want to hold an event here to make money. I wanted to have my dad's sixty-fifth birthday party here."

Don't bite, he ordered himself, but then just like a fish circling, he couldn't resist, even though he knew there might be a hook buried in the bait. "Why here? Your father has probably experienced every wonder the world has to offer."

"Exactly! My dad *has* seen everything in the entire world. But I just knew he'd never seen anything like this."

She looked out at the immensity of the sky. Her face was unguarded for a moment. Wistful.

The problem with a woman like her was that she could make a man weak when he most wanted to be strong. She could make him lean toward a temptation, even when he was aware there might be a hook buried in it.

"You can stay the night," he said coolly. "I don't want you attempting the roads in the dark."

"How thoughtful," she said snippily.

"Not really. I don't have the manpower to be staging a rescue if you go off the road."

"I'm quite capable of tackling the roads."

He heard something in her tone that made him suspect she was not quite as confident as she wanted to appear. "The deer and elk are out at night."

He saw something flicker in her face. What was he doing? What did he care if she got in her little toy car and drove away and he never saw her again?

He *cared.* Already. Even though he was irritated. Which just meant it was wiser—imperative, even—to send her on her way. In the morning.

"Bears come out at night."

She glanced around the yard warily, as if a bear might be hiding behind the tree swing. "I'll leave first thing in the morning."

"Animals are worse in the morning. At dawn."

"So, since you need to be in control of the whole world, when do you want me to leave?"

Control. The one thing a man doesn't really have, no matter what illusions he harbors. Still, he would do his best to protect her while she was in his domain.

"After breakfast would work."

"Are you inviting me for breakfast?"

"I'm feeding you. There's a difference."

"Fine."

"Good."

And yet, as he got up from the rocking chair and went into the house, snapping the screen door shut behind him with a little more force than was strictly necessary, Sam was aware he didn't feel *good* at all.

He had found solace from his grief in hard work. His business ventures benefitted from his single-minded drive to escape the pain of a loss he had not been able to control. He was more successful than he had ever been, and if it exhausted him, he saw that as a good thing. He always fell asleep the minute his head hit the pillow. But tonight, he tossed and turned, and the weariness did not work in his favor. Fences tumbled down and Sam thought of what he least wanted to think about.

He thought of Beth. He recognized he was still angry with his wife even though it was closing in on two years since she was gone. How could she do this to him? He knew getting sick was not her fault, and that made his resentment even more shameful. But he felt abandoned, left alone with a pile of broken dreams and a little girl to raise.

It pierced the ire how much he missed her. Wasn't the anger—like so much of his life—really about keeping the sorrow at bay? He missed her when he was raising Hannah, and on those special days, like Christmas and birthdays, but he especially missed her in moments like this one.

Moments that called for something more than he had to give. Qualities he thought of as feminine. Empathy. Intuition.

And suddenly, Sam knew Beth would be disappointed in him, and in the way he had handled all of this.

Shelby had driven all this way to try and make him see something. That she—a woman with access to anything—wanted to do something special for her dad, to give him something he had never had.

She *had* helped Sam out of a tough spot, and he was pretty sure it was the circumstances that had prevented her from telling him earlier that she wasn't from International Nanny Services.

He suddenly remembered Shelby telling them she had lost her mom, too.

Was it possible he wanted to get rid of her because of how she was making him *feel*, rather than anything she'd done?

Beth had always required him to be a better man. He knew he needed to be the best man he could be to raise his daughter. In these circumstances, what did that mean?

It meant he didn't repay Shelby's kindness in taking Hannah under her wing when he was in a pinch by being rude and selfish. By protecting himself at a cost to someone else.

It meant maybe he needed to apologize. He hoped it didn't mean he had to rethink his decision about the old timber-frame barn. Because that meant his life would be tangled with hers for longer. And look at how he *felt* after just a few hours of her acquaintance.

Tumultuous. Self-doubting. Insensitive. In danger.

When the first fingers of dawn began to paint his bedroom a faint blush, he gave up on sleeping. Sam felt as if he hadn't slept a wink. Hannah was not up yet.

He got up, showered and dressed, went down to the kitchen. Beth had designed it to her exacting standards. It reminded him those standards applied to him today.

Be a better man.

Buckie slammed a coffee cup down in front of him as soon as he entered the room. He glared at him.

"She's leaving," he told Sam.

Sam wondered if Shelby had been as restless as he, and if that was why she was up so early.

"Yeah, I know."

"Hannah likes her. I like her."

"She's not who she said she was."

"Anybody who can't tell who that girl is from lookin' in her eyes is just plain dumb."

"She likes to be called a woman. And she's not a nanny," Sam said tightly. "She came to rent the old barn for an event. After I'd already told her no."

"For her *dad*," Buckie said.

Jeez, had Shelby confided her whole life story in Buckie? What time *had* she gotten up? The sun was barely out of bed.

"Where is she right now?" He said this carelessly, as if he didn't care, except that she might be getting into trouble somewhere with her city ways. Getting her shoes stuck in the mud. Trying to pet the bull.

"She said she was going to go look at it."

"The barn? I don't know why she would. I told her no."

"Yeah, well, she said she wouldn't rent it from you now if her life depended on it."

"Quite the little tête–à–tête you two managed to have this morning," he said sourly.

"Just 'cause you speak French doesn't make you a class act," Buckie told him. "I know some French, too."

He said several words he must have learned from French sailors. Even though he massacred the accent, and Sam did not speak French, his meaning was abundantly clear.

This was the problem with having staff who had been around since before you were born, and who had wiped your nose and fussed over your bruises. No respect.

"You can't say stuff like that with a child in the house," Sam admonished him.

"You grew up on stuff like that. It didn't seem to hurt you."

"A *girl*," Sam reminded him.

"She ain't even up yet."

"Don't let that fool you. If you whispered *ice cream* right now, she'd be down here in three seconds."

Buckie just glared at him, as if he thought the possibility of Sam being a better man was pretty much hopeless. Then he turned and stirred a briskly bubbling pot. Porridge. Sam hated porridge. It smelled like it was scorching.

"She'll be staying for breakfast before she's on her way," Sam said, shamelessly vying for a change in menu. Buckie could—and often did—produce cuisine as good or better than five-star restaurants Sam had dined in.

"She grabbed a yogurt and an apple and said that was all she wanted."

It looked as if Buckie had made enough porridge to last a long, long time.

Sam told himself it was to appease Buckie and to get out of eating that porridge—nine days old just like the rhyme said, if the size of the pot was any indication—that he went in search of Shelby. But he knew that wasn't the whole truth.

Not even close.

It wasn't all about being a better man, either.

He found her sitting cross-legged in the very center of the old barn. She had opened both the front- and back-facing doors. She was facing the back view, the valley dazzling as the first rays of sun pierced the heavy morning mist that had settled over it.

He froze for a moment, watching the light spill around her, play with the curve of her neck, the roundness of her shoulders, the slender, straight line of her back. Her hair was wet and that turned it a shade darker, more golden.

He cleared his throat and she froze, then turned, a half-eaten apple in her hand.

Buckie had been right. Sam could see who she was in those amazing gold-green eyes.

"Don't get up," he said, when she scrambled to find her feet. She hesitated, then sank back down.

"Don't worry," she said, her voice tight, "I'm leaving. I'd be gone except I thought I should wait for the bears to get off the road. And say goodbye to Hannah."

Did she have to make him feel like more of a jerk by being thoughtful? Hannah would be upset if their visitor left without saying goodbye.

"Do you mind if I join you?"

She lifted a shoulder and he walked over to her. The stuffy suit from yesterday was gone. She was wearing black, formfitting yoga pants and a sleeveless white tank top. Sneakers had replaced the impractical heels.

It was obvious from her ease at sitting on the hard concrete floor that she did yoga. That probably explained her getting into the tent in Hannah's room, too.

A bra strap, impossibly white, was visible on one shoulder. For some reason, it made his mouth go dry. She shot him a look as he lowered himself to the floor beside her, making a manly effort not to groan.

He noticed that the indescribably beautiful smell of a woman in the morning wafted off her.

She glanced at him. His efforts to hide his discomfort did not succeed, because she smiled, though it seemed reluctant.

He was not sure he was strong enough to handle the smile *and* the enchantment of the morning light caressing her.

"You're more used to sitting on a horse," she concluded.

"You're right. Plus, there are lots of old injuries."

"From what?"

"Like every young guy who grows up around here, I had to try my hand at rodeo."

"Oh my," she said, sounding way too impressed.

"It's like wrestling calves. Not romantic."

Why did he have to keep using that word around her?

"Anyway, I sucked," he said. "I'm lucky I'm not in a wheelchair. For a sport that's so dangerous, it's really underpaid."

Get it over with, he instructed himself firmly, *then go*.

"You were right about the animals," she said. At his look of puzzlement, she passed him her phone. "The deer come out in the morning."

He smiled when he saw she had captured a shot of four cow elk, their bellies round with unborn calves, looking up from the new, dew-encrusted grass that sprouted in front of the barn. Their gazes on her were alert and curious. They didn't look at all nervous, as if they, too, could see who she really was.

He passed her back the phone. Their hands touched. He could feel the jolt up to his shoulder.

"They're elk," he said. "Not deer."

"Oh! City slicker mistake." She studied her phone for a moment.

"I wanted to tell you I'm sorry," he said gruffly. "I overreacted last night."

"I understand how it must feel like the biggest job in the world to protect Hannah."

He was silent, not wanting her to know how her *seeing* that, how her easy forgiveness, touched him.

"I'm to blame, too," she said. "I shouldn't have come here after you said no."

CHAPTER SEVEN

SAM RESISTED THE desire to agree with Shelby. She shouldn't have come here.

"I've held a lot of events," she went on, her voice low. "And in some pretty spectacular places. But from the moment I first saw this, I *felt* something. It's magnificent, but solid, too. It's like the past and the future are combined here. I felt as if this building was telling me what it wanted. It's even better up close. So many places disappoint when you see them for real, but not this one. It's better than anything I could have imagined."

She stopped. She blushed. She looked away from him. "I'm sorry. I'm gushing. You probably think I'm silly."

He was silent for a bit. He realized the silence was oddly comfortable between them, as if they had known each other longer than they actually had.

"My wife felt the same way about it," he said, reluctantly. "From the minute Beth first saw it, she started planning, *seeing* how it could be. She, too, had a vision of holding gatherings here. She thought of invitation-only events, with the best food, world-renowned musicians, celebrations of friends and family. She was eventually going to build a permanent kitchen in a separate building. She was a chef. Bethany Britannia."

"Oh my goodness. I watched her on television. I ate in her restaurant in Paris once. It was sublime. I'm so sorry for your loss. And Hannah's."

Just words, but it felt, again, as if his fences were coming down. He, of all people, knew the danger of downed fences, but still, he engaged when he should have been disengaging.

"Yours, too," he said. "You told Hannah your mom died."

A shadow crossed the loveliness of her features.

"It was a long time ago, though I still feel I know exactly how Hannah feels. There's something about losing the person who loves you best of all that it's hard to heal from. Especially when you're young. I wasn't as young as Hannah though. I was ten."

Sam wanted to say he also loved Hannah best of all, but he knew, no matter what he did, it would never be the same as a mother's love.

"It was like my dad tried to shield me from life, after that. To make up for it, somehow."

He could hear affection in her voice for her father's efforts. And he could also hear that it had been a failure. Which he filed in the *notes to self* compartment of his brain.

"What happened to your mom?"

She hesitated. "It was a car accident. Even as shielded as I was, there were whispers around it. I think there's lots I don't know. And here I am, eighteen years later, still not wanting to find out."

"I'm sorry," he said, and found he meant it from the bottom of his heart.

"What happened to Bethany?" she asked softly.

He never talked about it. Part of the reason he had retreated to the ranch was because he didn't have to. This was a society of men, and they did not talk about their broken hearts.

And yet it suddenly felt compelling to do just that.

"After Hannah was born, Beth realized something wasn't quite right. She didn't want to tell me, because I'd lost both my parents that year. She—we—waited too long. By the time she got a diagnosis, it was too late."

"Oh, Sam." Somehow, her hand was on his arm.

Just as he could see who she was in her eyes, he could feel who she was in that touch. Stronger than she looked. Compassionate. Empathetic.

"So much loss," she said. The words were simple. And yet so heartfelt.

"What are the dates for the birthday party?" he said, sliding his arm out from under her hand before he was tempted to lay his head on her shoulder and drink in the comfort she offered.

Shelby tried not to flinch when Sam pulled his arm away from her touch.

Suddenly, what she had wanted most—this barn as a venue—faded. She could feel the danger in the air.

Not just in how she had felt when he sat beside her, his long legs stretched out in front of him, not just how she had felt when she touched his arm, but how she felt now.

As if she wanted to be with him.

To tell him things. *I don't really remember my mom. How do I know if she loved me best of all?* It had actually felt strange saying that, that her mother loved her best of all, as if it was a lie.

Something snaked along her spine, a realization that the secrets around her mother—the things she could not remember, which was pretty much everything before age ten—was what kept her from wanting the things other people wanted: families, children, commitment. She shivered.

Why was being here, just for this short time, making her feel as if the past she had managed to outrun was catching up with her?

All kinds of danger lurked here.

And maybe the worst one was the desire to be needed. Whatever she had felt in her childhood, it had not been that. She had not felt, even after the death of her mother, needed. Isn't that what most families did? Leaned on each other, needed each other, to get through bad times?

Really, the first time she'd ever felt needed was when she had put together the wedding for Kylie. And her business had made her feel that way ever since.

But compared to the needs of Sam and Hannah, it felt superficial.

She wanted to help him heal. To be the one who made him laugh again, and live again. To help Hannah. It felt as if that desire to tangle her life with theirs was intensifying. As if, in some deep way, the part of herself she had lost when she was ten lay in this direction.

And this direction only.

On the other hand, wouldn't she be the worst possible person to think she had anything to offer anyone else? Her whole life had been an avoidance strategy.

Better to get away from the temptation to leave her map for life behind and take an unmarked road. Better to get away from Sam Waters and his adorable daughter, and the enchantment of this ranch and especially this building they now sat in.

She had a plan for life—since aversion to commitment had been solidly cemented into place even before her last fiasco with Keith—Eventually was going to be her whole life. It was going to fill every need in her, satisfy her, give her a

sense of belonging and accomplishment and ful-
fillment.

A commitment to a business, and all her plans
for it and her life, felt so safe.

Sam Waters was the kind of man who left plans
like that in a burnt pile of smoldering ash.

"I was planning his party for the first weekend
in September. But it's okay," she said, inserting a
breezy note into her voice, "I decided last night
I'd find a different place for it."

Juggling her half-eaten apple, she scrolled
through her phone. "I understand the concern
you voiced about disruptions to the ranch routine. I imagine you would have felt those were
more manageable if it was your wife doing the
event. I can also understand your reluctance to let
someone outside of the community use it when
it meant so much to Bethany."

Not to mention she would now feel an added
pressure to do Bethany Britannia's vision justice.

She found the photo she was looking for and
held it up for him to see. "It's a vineyard. Tus-
cany."

He regarded it, his brow furrowed.

"Buckie told me you wouldn't rent from me
now if your life depended on it."

Her life—or at least her life as she knew it—
did feel as if it depended on *not* going any further
down this road. She scrambled to her feet—be-

fore he got up first and offered her his hand, again—and dusted herself off.

He got to his feet, too. He winced. "I might need to take a few yoga lessons from you."

Wouldn't that be fun? she thought.

Without the high heels, Sam was taller than her by a head. So broad across the shoulders and narrow at the waist. He looked incredible this morning in a pressed white shirt, his legs long and lean in dark denim jeans. There was something about his polished cowboy boots that was undeniably sexy.

She had the entirely inappropriate thought that she wanted to step not away from him, but into him. That she wanted to wrap her arms around his waist and lay her head on his chest, and tell him all those thoughts she had just had.

That she would help him through it.

That he would help her.

That together they would help each other.

That she did not really remember her mother, let alone whether she had loved her best of all.

Stop, Shelby ordered herself, with desperate firmness. *Just stop indulging these fantasies. That one man and one woman could take on the world.*

Instead of stepping into him, she stuck out her hand, all business. She couldn't let him see how frazzled she felt. She realized she still had a half-eaten apple in her hand. She looked around and then stuffed it in her back pocket.

"Nice to meet you," she said formally, offering her apple-sticky hand. "I'll go say goodbye to Hannah and be on my way. Hopefully the elk are off the road. And the bears. Imagine the damage one of them could do to my little toy car."

She was aware she was babbling. Trying to outrun something. He wasn't taking her hand. No doubt because of the apple, not because of the electricity. Maybe she was the only one who felt it. Maybe she was like this woman who hadn't been touched in so long that a bump of hands practically made her swoon with longing... She was babbling inwardly now.

"What if I didn't rent it to you?"

"Sorry?" She let her hand awkwardly drop away.

"Shelby, what if you stayed?"

It was unfair how her name sounded coming off Sam's lips, she thought. It was unfair how his words stirred some deep longing in her.

To just see.

Where it could go. Where the unexpected could take her.

"You know," she said, noting her voice sounded high and squeaky, "I really can't. I have a business to run. We're putting finishing details on a debutante ball right now. Who knew that such a thing still existed? I've secured a refurbished mansion in Mississippi for it."

She let her voice drift away. Babble. Babble. Babble. She had *never* been a babbler.

For a moment he didn't say anything, and she jumped into the silence. "Besides, I didn't pack for a stay. I have no clothes to wear. Look what I'm wearing today. My gym clothes."

His eyes flicked to her, moved away, but not before she saw she was not the only one feeling the electricity.

All the more reason for him to jump on her excuses.

Though she wished he would jump on—where had that thought come from? She didn't just need to get out of here, she needed to get out of here at top speed. She needed to act as if she was the fox and the hounds were at her heels.

Sam lifted his shoulder, as if *no clothes* was nothing. She noticed, again, how broad it was. She wondered how no clothes would look on him.

She hoped she wasn't blushing.

"It's quite pressing that I leave," she squeaked. Pressing. As in them, pressing together, the hard lines of his body up against hers, with no space between them.

"I was hoping we could negotiate a trade," he said, oblivious, thankfully, to the wayward ways of her mind.

"A trade?" Again, her voice had that odd squeaky

note to it, and her mind was negotiating all kinds of trades. Mostly involving lips. She tried to think if she had ever had this visceral a reaction to a man. Her mind was blank.

"If you could help me with Hannah for the next ten days, until calving is over, and I have some business trips out of the way—that would be the Sunday following the grad event—I'll give you the barn to use for your father's birthday."

He'd give her the barn! It was a gift! Why did she feel compelled to talk him out of it?

"It's probably just not a good idea. I mean, I have friends with kids, but other than that my experience is zero. You need a qualified nanny."

"I've tried the experts. All their so-called experience didn't seem worth a whit. I think you could muddle through."

"You want to trust your child to a complete amateur?"

"Everybody's a complete amateur at kids," he said softly. "You should see how it feels the first time you hold your baby."

The stab of longing Shelby—the one who had never wanted children—felt was nothing short of shocking.

It was another clue of what needed to be done. *Say no.*

Of course she had to say no! A week? With this man? And his precious daughter? It could change the well-planned course of her whole life! It could change her belief system! She had just felt a stab of longing to hold a baby! If that wasn't a warning, what was?

But the barn itself seemed to be whispering to her. As was the mist-shrouded valley beyond it. As she watched, before her very eyes, the sun came out with force and the mist burned off.

And she could see so clearly.

"Hannah likes you," he said softly.

Everything in her weakened.

Why not say yes?

She had Marcus now, her assistant. The details for the debutante ball were nearly completed. She had a phone. She could still be there, virtually.

She also had to admit that the ball seemed suddenly frivolous in light of Sam's proposal.

Proposal. The whole English language now seemed rife with double meanings. But Shelby was so aware it wasn't really Sam's proposal—suggestion—that she was saying yes or no to.

It was the absolute adventure of life, with all its twists and turns and its propensity for the unexpected, its seeming delight in leading an unsuspecting traveler down dark paths and through unknown woods, where everything you thought you knew would be challenged and where your destination could equally hold danger or enchantment.

It was the type of decision someone should take time to think about. Time in absolute solitude, if possible, like a monk deciding whether or not to take a final vow. It was not a decision that should be made in such close proximity of an unfairly attractive man, in a barn that was putting a spell on her. Or maybe that was the unfairly attractive man.

But *I need time to consider my options* is not what came out of Shelby's mouth. Not even close.

"Yes," she whispered.

CHAPTER EIGHT

Sam's smile was the very same as the mist burning off the valley—as if something that had always been there was suddenly revealed—and it was so beautiful it was nearly soul shattering.

They walked back to the house together, Shelby aware of the easy grace and strength in his stride, how much taller than her he was, how one misstep could cause their shoulders to touch. She was aware of how the morning suddenly had a shine to it that could not be fully explained by the burning off of the mist or the surprising strength of the spring sunshine.

"You can toss what's left of that apple," he said.

"I was going to wait for a garbage can." She made a note to herself: he noticed everything.

"Those *deer* you saw this morning would like it. I should probably show you a picture of a bear so you don't think it's the cutest big dog you ever saw."

She smiled. He was *teasing* her. And she didn't need any more coaxing than that. She fished the chewed core out of her pocket and dropped it on the ground.

As they entered the kitchen, she saw Hannah was at the table, her hair adorably sleep tangled. She was in pink, fuzzy pajamas with feet in them that could almost make someone who had sworn off children of her own reconsider.

Why, exactly, was she so adverse?

"Daddy," Hanna cried, as if Sam was returning from the wars. She got up and flew to him. He hoisted her up with ease, planted a kiss on her nose and set her down, trying to hide the obvious consternation her tangled hair was causing him.

It was clear that Sam loved Hannah best of all, and that the little girl was completely secure in that knowledge.

Boswell had never been demonstrative. There had been an awkward hug every now and then, a kiss on the cheek, a pat on the shoulder.

Never this, that she could remember, an unspoken action that said *you are my world, my reason.*

She could not remember her mother being demonstrative, either. Wasn't that the sort of thing you should remember?

There was that voice again, from the shadows, a little girl, her past self, watching her carefully. Had Shelby been her mother's world? Her reason?

The question—the fact she was asking herself questions like this, and even reconsidering her beliefs about having children—was disturbing. What had she let herself in for?

"Shelby's going to stay for a bit," Sam said. "Just to help out around here until calving is done and the grad event is over."

There was, wisely, no mention of that help being Hannah related.

Shelby had the odd feeling the announcement about her staying might have actually been for Buckie's benefit, as much as Hannah's, because a look she couldn't quite decipher passed between the two men.

"What's for breakfast?" Sam asked, casually.

"Buckie is making us mouse pancakes," Hannah said.

"Mouse pancakes?" Shelby teased, shaking off her own shadows. "I cannot eat a mouse! And I don't care if it does make me a city girl!"

Hannah chortled. "No, the pancakes aren't made out of mice! Ugh! They're shaped like Mickey!"

As Shelby watched, the cook took a big pot off the stove and scraped its mushy contents into a pail.

"What's that?" she asked.

"Just mash for an orphaned calf," Buckie said, but he shot Sam a look.

"Oh! An orphan!" Hannah said happily. Apparently this was ranch life, because the child did not seem the least saddened by the circumstances that brought about an orphan. "Can we go see it? Shelby, do you want to?"

"Sure, if that's what you'd like to do."

It occurred to her that Hannah had accepted that Shelby's role would be childcare.

Shelby shot Sam a look. The relief on his face was palpable. He did a gesture with his hands, which she took to mean *can you manage the hair?* She nodded, and his look of pleasure made her feel as if she would do anything for him.

She was getting in deeper and deeper.

It was because he was a daddy, not because he was just about the most attractive man she had ever laid eyes on.

"I'll have regular pancakes," Sam said, sitting down at the head of the table. Shelby took the seat beside Hannah.

But when Buckie put a big platter of pancakes on the table, they were all mouse pancakes. Even though she had already eaten, Shelby couldn't resist taking one of them.

It took up her whole plate, with its two smaller round circles for ears and one large one for the face.

Hannah showed her how to make the features come alive with chocolate wafer cookies for eyes and a string of liquorice for the mouth.

"Isn't this a special occasion kind of breakfast?" Sam asked.

"It is a special occasion," Buckie said. "We got company."

Sam considered that for a moment, then cast her a glance. Then to Hannah's—and Shelby's—delight, he surrendered. He took the cookies and carefully added eyes to his pancake. Not satisfied with that, he made liquorice eyelashes.

"Ha," Buckie said, wandering over to regard Sam's handiwork. "This work of art from the person who wanted regular pancakes."

And this enjoyment, Shelby added silently, putting a mouth on her mouse, *from the person who didn't want children*.

When they finished decorating mouse faces on their pancakes, they all admired each other's masterpieces. And then Hannah picked up a spray can of whipped cream from the middle of the table and obliterated the face her father had made on his pancake.

"Take that," she said, gleeful.

"Oh, yeah?" Sam replied. He grabbed the whipped cream from her, but then turned to Shelby and the face on her mouse pancake disappeared under a blob of cream. "Take that."

Hannah chortled with absolute and fiendish delight.

Spitting with equal parts of indignation and laughter, Shelby tried to grab the whipped cream from him, but he was too fast. He leaned away from her. She leaned harder, but he got up from his chair and moved away, holding it high. She had no choice but to follow him.

"You wrecked my mouse!"

"It's not personal," he said. "It's a tradition!"

Shelby backed him into a corner, and then made a leap to grab the whipped cream. Just for a moment, the movement pressed her full against him. It was just as she'd imagined it when that word *pressed* had crossed her lips earlier. Sam Waters was all heat and hard lines and male strength. At the moment, the fact that he was a daddy was the least important thing about him.

It had felt so easy to fall toward the comfortable domestic routines of the household. But now, she could feel an underlying tension, a sizzle that had nothing to do with mouse pancakes! Which was more dangerous to her commitment to non-commitment?

He stared at her, and his grip loosened on the whipped cream spray can. She grabbed it, wanting to make the moment light, to disperse the intensity of it.

She aimed the spray can straight at him, the way Hannah had aimed the doll at her yesterday.

He put his arms up in surrender. She giggled. As soon as she did, he dropped his arms and caught the wrist of her hand that was holding the whipped cream.

She pressed down the nozzle. Her shot went wild and whipped cream squirted onto his cheek.

For a moment, the whole kitchen went very still at her obviously crossed boundary. He let go of her arm.

"Take that," Shelby said, and Buckie and Hannah roared with laughter.

Sam wiped the blob from his cheek and licked it off his fingers. Way too slowly. He gave her a look that somehow seemed loaded and very personal, indeed. It felt, suddenly, as if the two of them were all alone in the kitchen.

But the sizzling look was only a distraction because, just as his fake surrender had been, quick as lightning, he took the spray can from her. For a moment, he seemed to consider his options.

His gaze let her know what he could do with the whipped cream. And maybe wanted to. But he turned on his heel, went back to the table and squirted cream on Hannah's mouse pancake.

"Take that," he said. Then, he grabbed his own pancake off his plate, folded it in half like a sandwich, and took a bite. With his other hand he took his cowboy hat off the back door, grabbed a briefcase, and was gone, the screen door snapping quietly shut behind him.

"A briefcase?" Shelby said.

Buckie snorted. "You didn't think those was going-to-work-cows clothes, did you?"

Actually, she had, but now that she thought about it, that crisp white shirt and the polished boots probably were not cowhand clothes.

Buckie sat down with them, and regarded the mess of whipped cream nearly obliterating the pancakes.

"It's our tradition," Buckie explained to Shelby. "We decorate the pancakes then we whip cream-bomb each other's. We've done that since he was a little boy."

The big cook's features softened, remembering Sam as a child. Shelby could see that though this house had been hit by way too much tragedy, the love was so strong here. It was holding them up, whether they knew it or not.

Shelby had had so many spectacular moments in her life that she probably could not count them all. She'd had many moments that other people could not even imagine. She'd swooped down slopes on skis, snorkeled the most famous reef in the world, ridden in some of the world's rarest and most fancy sports cars.

She had dined at five-star restaurants, been to charity balls in palaces, been to movie openings with the actors who had starred in them.

How could this moment of pancakes and laughter and flying whipped cream—being part of a silly family tradition—feel as if it was the best one she had ever had?

In Shelby's world, had there been love to hold her up when she needed it? Of course, her father had loved her, in his awkward way. Of that, she had no doubt.

But she was aware a door that she kept tightly closed had opened a crack. Where had her mother been when she needed love? Why was that whole part of her life shrouded in darkness?

She wrestled that door firmly shut.

And thought instead about the layer of tension between her and Sam. That definitely fell outside of the perimeters of family tradition, and yet it was part of the light that infused the day and the moment.

What had Sam felt when they had made full-on body contact like that?

Something.

Otherwise, why would he have left so suddenly?

"Well, well, well," Buckie said enigmatically. "It's good to see the boss laugh."

That made her feel guilty for telling Sam joy was a topic he knew nothing about.

Buckie looked at Shelby for a moment, then turned away, whistling tunelessly, and trying to hide his smile.

"Do you know how to make braids?" Hannah asked, as they finished up their absolutely delicious pancakes.

She felt a little smug. Sam had indicated hair was an issue, but Hannah was already trusting her with it!

Even though she was not a kid person, she had been a kid once!

"I used to have a doll, a little bigger than the

one you shot me with yesterday, and that was my favorite thing to do with her. Should we try it on you? Do you think you'd like a single plait down your back, or two braids?"

"On me?" Hannah said, wide-eyed. "I was thinking of Rascal!"

Buckie snorted with enjoyment over Hannah's misunderstanding.

"On you," Shelby confirmed.

Hannah considered this. "I guess we could try," she said, but without much enthusiasm.

"Girl things," Buckie muttered with approval, waving off Shelby's offer to help clean up the kitchen.

Hannah's bedroom was fit for a princess. Aside from the delightful tent for reading, it had a twin bed with a pink canopy, a window seat filled with plump pillows and stuffed toys, and shelves and shelves of books.

Shelby was willing to bet Sam hadn't had much to do with the design and planning of the room.

The room had an adjoining bathroom and Shelby convinced Hannah—with lots of bubbles—to get into the tub. She gave the mop of hair a thorough washing, and added lots of conditioner to detangle it.

She wondered why she had avoided children so scrupulously all her adult life. There was something very lovely about their trust and innocence.

Hannah's thick, curly hair was gorgeous. And

an utter mess. It had been surface controlled for a long time.

"Let's put on some music," Shelby said, after Hannah was out of the tub and wrapped in a big white towel. She got out her phone. "Who do you like?"

Hannah named the pre-teen popstar of the day, and Shelby found it on her phone, and they sang along as she worked her way through that glorious head of hair. When she was done, a single thick plait fell over Hannah's shoulder, tied with a ribbon Shelby had stolen from one of the teddy bears on the window seat.

Together, they picked out an outfit for the day: bright yellow shorts with a top covered in drawings of lemon drops. Rather than fighting her, Hannah seemed to be lapping up the feminine input. Then they went to visit the orphaned calf and both were allowed to feed it milk from a bottle.

Again, she was aware the experience was enriched by sharing it with a child.

"He's very greedy," Shelby said, when it took all her strength to keep the calf from pulling the bottle right out of her hands with his desperate sucking.

Rascal was in a stall in the same barn as the calf, nickering softly at them.

"He wants a cookie," Hannah said.

They fed the tiny horse—who was at least as greedy as the calf—cookies and then brushed him.

"Can you show me how to braid?"

Shelby showed Hannah and soon the pony was sporting a clumsy new hairstyle that he seemed—if the shaking of his head was any indication—less thrilled with than his owner was.

Shelby was shocked by how the morning had evaporated. After the whipped cream incident, she had felt a tension—she didn't want to call it hopefulness—about seeing Sam, but she had not seen him, and eventually the tension of that expectation dissipated.

She reminded herself this experience had a ten-day time limit, and so she gave herself over to exploring this new world of the ranch through the wondrous eyes of a child.

Hannah delighted in everything. Not just big things like the orphaned calf and her pony, but ladybugs and new leaves and the color of dandelions, which she demonstrated made a really nice stain.

"Look! I can use dandelion juice to make my hands match my shorts!"

"Dandelion juice and mouse pancakes. I'm not sure about life on the ranch."

"I won't make you drink any if you let me dye your hands, too."

What choice did a person have, really, when it was put like that? And so, she let Hannah dye her hands, the little girl's tongue caught between her teeth with her intensity of focus.

Shelby felt a stirring of incredible wonder as Hannah stepped back from her work, and Shelby looked at her yellow-dyed hands. It felt as if she was having childhood experiences that she had missed.

Had she missed them, or were they part of what she could not remember?

CHAPTER NINE

SHELBY DECIDED NOT to spoil these delight-infused moments being given to her with too much contemplations.

After they had finally managed to scrub the dandelion stains off their hands, she and Hannah sat down with Alvin on the wraparound porch to a delicious lunch of thick roast beef sandwiches on homemade bread.

"Oh, look, dandelion juice!" Hannah declared of the hand-squeezed lemonade. She laughed fiendishly when Shelby looked at her glass with pretend trepidation. "And we're having lizard juice with supper, aren't we, Buckie?"

"Fresh out of lizards," Buckie said. "Maybe tomorrow. By the way, Hannah, your hair looks really pur-ty." The little girl preened.

Again, Shelby felt the love that surrounded Hannah.

In Shelby's various households, there was a preference, unspoken as it might have been, that the staff remain as invisible as possible. She liked that Alvin seemed to be more a member of the family than an employee. Shelby noticed neither the cook nor Hannah seemed to be expecting Sam.

After lunch, Hannah fetched a storybook—they seemed to be all over the house, which Shelby loved—and they curled up together on one of the deeply cushioned rattan sofas on the deck.

The little girl snuggled deeper into her as she read.

Shelby had had a nanny who liked to read to her, but didn't recall Boswell ever reading to her. Had her mother? Surely you would remember sweet moments like the one she was experiencing right now, forever. So, why didn't she?

Despite a ceiling fan lazily moving air around the porch, it was unseasonably warm. A fat bee buzzed by. Hannah's head drooped, and then she slumped against Shelby's midriff. A gentle snore came from her, and then saliva pooled on Shelby's top.

She felt her own eyes grow heavy as contentment enveloped her like the hug of a weighted blanket.

She woke up when Hannah stirred against her. Her tank top and her yoga pants were sticking to her. Hannah looked flushed. Her hair was stuck to the sides of her face.

"I'm hot," Hannah said, plucking at her yellow

shorts. And then she brightened. "We should play water blaster."

We.

How quickly that had happened. The child's quick trust and their comfort with each other, seeing the world through Hannah's eyes.

"What's water blaster?"

"I have these blasters that you fill with water and you squirt each other. And you run through the sprinkler at the same time. You get *really* soaked."

"That sounds much more amazing than only getting partly soaked, but I don't have a bathing suit."

"You don't need a real bathing suit. Just a pair of shorts and a top."

"I don't have shorts, either."

"If I find you a pair, will you play water blaster with me?"

Really, given the heat of the day, the clinging yoga pants, and Hannah's sweet pleading, it was too tempting to resist. "All right."

Hannah disappeared into the house and Shelby looked over the landscape and contemplated the surprise life had given her. It had not only brought her to the ranch, but had also given her the gift of a perfect day.

Well, except for shadowy memories and questions.

Still, how long had it been since she had experienced a day that was not planned? How long since she had a go-with-the-flow kind of day?

Hannah came back after a while, in a one-piece bathing suit. She held two large purple contraptions that looked as if they would hold a gallon of water each, and a pair of shorts.

"Here," she said happily, handing the shorts to Shelby.

It wasn't until she was holding them that she realized Hannah had handed her a pair of men's boxers. Obviously way too small to be the cook's.

Which meant they could only belong to one person, which also answered the age-old question: boxers or briefs?

She realized—not that she had thought about it, but that if she had—this was not quite what she would have expected for Sam's choice of undies.

She would not have expected playful. And yet, there it was. Bright pink shorts with green fish all over them.

"Where did you get these?"

"Daddy's drawer. I knew my shorts wouldn't fit you. Buckie helped me pick them for him for Christmas."

So, they weren't Sam's style. A novelty item. He had probably never worn them. Which somehow made the fact she was touching them less intense.

"I'm not sure I should wear your daddy's shorts." Actually, she was pretty sure she should not.

"Pleeaassee," Hannah said, leaning into her and blinking adorably.

How could she resist that? Or the pull of playing in a sprinkler on a hot afternoon? It was such an ordinary thing to do, and yet Shelby was so aware it was among the many ordinary childhood things she had never done—or at least, couldn't remember doing.

She went into a bathroom off the porch, pulled off the yoga pants and put on the shorts. She left on the tank top.

She was pretty sure she looked like a tourist in Hawaii, baggy-bottomed and white-legged.

But it didn't matter one little bit.

When she emerged from the bathroom, Hannah handed her a "weapon" and led her onto the rolling expanse of lush green grass in the backyard. Already squealing with anticipation, she went and turned on the tap that was connected to the hose.

A fan of water shot out of the sprinkler, which began oscillating back and forth.

"Look, rainbows," Hannah shouted excitedly, abandoning the water blasters. "Pretend we're at a horse show, Shelby, and we're jumping rainbows."

Hannah led, galloping through the lines of water. Shelby should have known from Hannah's shout just how cold the water was going to be, but it took her by surprise. She howled at the shock of the cold.

But then couldn't wait to turn around and do it again.

Soon, they had the water blasters filled up and were romping around the yard, in and out of the sprinkler, and squirting each other.

Shelby was not sure she had laughed so hard in her entire life.

Infused with their laughter and squeals of delight, an ordinary hot afternoon became a magical place of imaginary horses leaping over rainbows.

It became the childhood Shelby had never had.

Sam could hear them before he saw them. It was incredibly hot given that they were still days away from summer. His shirt was sticking to him after just a short walk up from the helicopter pad.

He'd had a good day in Calgary, signing off on a deal that had been in the works for months. He had been aware, though, of feeling preoccupied. Both eager and reluctant to head back to the ranch.

And this was the reason right here.

He could have avoided the commotion in the backyard and gone through the front door, but somehow he was drawn to the screams of laughter like a magnet drawn to steel.

He paused when he came around the corner of the house and saw them in the backyard.

Hannah and Shelby were totally unaware of him as they chased each other, water blasters in hand and shrieking with laughter, through the sprinkler.

His daughter had on her bathing suit. He noticed her hair was in a thick braid. But even the new, tidy hairstyle was totally eclipsed by her radiance, by the happiness pouring off of her. It had been a long time since he had seen Hannah give herself over to just having fun.

How had Shelby so effortlessly accomplished what he had not been able to?

His attention shifted.

If he was expecting to impersonally analyze Shelby's reason for success, he was in for a shock.

Sam felt his mouth go dry. Since the whipped cream incident this morning, he should have been prepared for the fact that cool-headed analysis had already gone out the window. Hadn't he already been having an awful time not feeling preoccupied with the new nanny, who was not a nanny at all?

Now, he could see there were some things that overrode a man's ability to be rational.

Shelby had given herself over to water play. As he watched, she gave her soaked head a shake and droplets flew off that honey-colored hair and cascaded around her. Water sluiced down her face. Her shout of pure enjoyment shivered along his spine.

Unlike his daughter, she was not wearing a

swimsuit. She was barefooted and long legged, like that filly that had been born this morning.

As he squinted at her, Sam was pretty sure she was wearing a pair of his underwear. Which seemed way too personal!

His underwear was plastered to her. So was that little white tank top she'd been wearing this morning.

It left very little to the imagination. The litheness of her body was completely outlined. The fabric of the tank top had become transparent. Underneath it was the lacy bra that he had glimpsed the white strap of earlier.

He felt, suddenly and embarrassingly, like a peeper. He turned to slide away and go in through the front door, after all.

"Daddy!"

Too late.

And here Hannah came, running on chubby legs, her braid flying behind her, her water blaster poised for attack.

Again, he was totally entranced by the look on Hannah's features. A man lived to see a look like that on his child's face.

"Take that," she said with glee, unloading most of the contents of the water blaster on him. She cackled happily. Shockingly, Shelby-in-his-shorts joined his daughter in the attack, racing up to him and blasting his face. Deliberately. Not a slip, like with that whipped cream this morning.

He held up his arms, but Shelby took aim at his hat, and knocked it right off his head.

"Hey! Didn't anyone tell you a man's cowboy hat is sacred?"

"I must have missed that part of the introductory tour."

Did that mean he should have given her a tour, instead of running out of the kitchen this morning as if his hair was on fire? It seemed it might have been the reasonable thing to do. He'd been a reasonable man his whole life.

Why did it suddenly feel as if reason was going out the window?

Hannah shot from below, and Shelby unloaded a stream of water down his shirt.

The cold water felt shockingly good. Reason be damned, retreat was out of the question. He pushed through his attackers, bent down and picked up the sprinkler. Armed, holding the sprinkler in front of him like a sword, he whirled back on them. They both ran.

He caught Hannah first, and held her under the spray while she wriggled and shrieked. His other attacker didn't let up the whole time, shooting him with her water blaster, going for the back of his neck, drenching his shoulders. He let go of Hannah, who collapsed on the ground laughing and turned on her.

Shelby darted out of his way. He ran after her, sprinkler in hand. Running was awkward in cowboy boots and it was slippery. She could have easily outrun him, except she was the one who lost her footing on the water-slick grass.

She went down, sliding through the grass, water blaster held out in front of her. She hit his hat at crushing speed. She was laughing so hard—especially after she hit the hat—that Sam was not sure how she could breathe.

"Don't," she begged, rolling over on her stomach, even as she continued to fire away at him with her water blaster. He was not sure why she would resist the sprinkler. It was not as if she could get any wetter, or any more see-through. He caught her ankle and held it. She tried to pull it away, but he directed the full force of the sprinkler at her.

The ribbons of water hit her and sluiced off of her. When she realized escape was futile, she gave herself over to it, arching her back, and opening her mouth to taste the droplets.

He was pretty sure he'd seen a movie with a scene like this.

It was much more erotic in person.

Some shocking wanting shot through him. He was not sure if she had planned this, but he dropped the sprinkler as if it had burned him. Hannah, thankfully totally unaware of his very adult reaction to Shelby, had been waiting for the opportunity. She swooped in and grabbed the abandoned sprinkler, giving chase around the yard.

Shelby didn't rejoin the game. Instead, she lay in the patch of sunlight, panting, her knees up, her arms thrown open.

Unaware she was a goddess. Or maybe she *was* aware, and deliberately tormenting him.

He fervently wished he could take back his own awareness.

"Ice pops," Buckie shouted from the porch. "Raspberry."

Hannah dropped the sprinkler and ran to the cook, who handed her a towel and the flavored ice-on-a-stick, before he went back in the house. Hannah wrapped herself in the towel and went around the side porch to sit down.

It made Sam feel oddly alone with Shelby who, with sensual grace born of what he assumed were long hours of yoga, unfolded herself and got up.

How was she making those shorts look like that? Shouldn't he address the fact he didn't want her wearing his shorts, and he certainly didn't want her rummaging around in his drawers. Had she gone in his drawers?

Gone in them. She *was* in his drawers.

"Hannah lent me your shorts," she said, adding mind reading to her list of superpowers. "I hope you don't mind."

He *did* mind. Sam was unfortunately aware it

would be churlish to say so. She'd already told him she didn't have any clothes here with her.

What was most important? She had made his daughter happy!

He was aware that his jeans were heavy and soaked and uncomfortable. His shirt, too. He was aware he certainly did not want to see Shelby's mouth closing around an ice pop, her luscious pink tongue darting out to catch drips.

He beat her to the porch, went in and let the door snap behind him. The house felt cool and dark, a sanctuary for rational people. He brushed by Buckie.

"You going to go through the house drippin' like that?" the cook asked, disapprovingly.

"No," Sam snapped, then added in an undertone, "I'm going to strip off right here in front of the whole world so I don't get puddles on your damned floor."

"Ain't nobody here but you and me," Buckie said mildly.

The man was being deliberately obtuse. "Somebody could be coming in for her damned ice pop."

Buckie backed up, eyes wide, hands up. "Hey, no need to get mad."

"I'm not mad."

No, he wasn't mad, but there was no denying the fire that was burning.

"Huh," Buckie said skeptically.

"Ice pops?" Sam said. Since Buckie thought

he was mad anyway, he might as well air all his grievances.

"What's wrong with ice pops?" Buckie asked, all innocence.

They both turned as Shelby approached. They could see her through the screen door, coming up the steps. She was wringing out her wet hair.

Watching her eat an ice pop would be X-rated, Sam thought.

Buckie gave him a smirk. Another damned mind reader on the property! With one final glare, Sam moved by him, dripping water the whole way.

Some more cold water was in order. *Tout de suite.* Not that knowing the odd French phrase made him a class act, as Buckie had so helpfully pointed out.

CHAPTER TEN

Sam took a long, cold shower and a miss on dinner. He was pretty sure Buckie would be having a good smirk over that, too.

As far as Shelby was concerned, Sam considered avoidance to be as good a strategy as any. In fact, four days later, like a prisoner marking his time, he found a pen and got ready to put one more highly satisfied X through a day on his calendar. He'd managed to find business away from the ranch for most of those days.

He had one last meeting in Calgary tomorrow, so that would be five down, five to go.

If his daughter had noticed he was leaving early and coming home late, she hadn't complained about it. Which, okay, hurt a bit, but Hannah knew the realities of ranch life. There had been lots of times before now she'd had to hang out in the kitchen with Buckie because the ranch—or one of his other businesses—needed attention.

The trade-off for not being missed was well worth it. From a distance, Sam made note of Hannah and Shelby, playing dress-up, building a house out of sticks in the wooded area behind the house, and having extravagant tea parties there. They read stories and drew pictures and did things with each other's hair. They were being girls.

Their laughter, their voices formed a backdrop to his days.

He couldn't help but notice that Shelby was playful, like a big kid, which was the only safe way to think about her. Her makeshift wardrobe accentuated that. Buckie had found a few pairs of small jeans somewhere, which she had to wear rolled up. The men's shirts she had to knot at the waist to keep them from going down to her knees.

The look, thankfully, was more Huck Finn than sexy farmgirl.

The heat was holding so there was, of course, the daily sprinkler escapade. He had made it a point not to join in, but word of the water fun had gone through the barn like wildfire. Sam had to forbid the hands from finding excuses to go up to the house in the heat of the day.

He had just finished the *X* when his phone pinged. Sam looked down at the message. It was an invitation for Hannah to have a playdate at the neighbor's. He glanced at his watch. Was she still up?

He opened his door a crack and listened to the sounds coming from the bedroom down the hall.

Shelby was still with her. He could hear them laughing.

He looked at the message again. Really, he should ask Hannah what she wanted to do. A playdate was a big deal when the nearest child Hannah's age lived twenty-five kilometers away. On the other hand, Shelby was with her. Maybe he should just make the decision.

He contemplated that. Avoidance was a fine strategy, but he was acting like a teenage boy who was scared of getting a hard-on in the presence of his crush.

Crush?

Okay, he had been watching her from afar, but *crush* was a little strong. This was simply what too much isolation did to a man. Too much avoidance.

Was he really at a point where he would put his Shelby-avoidance strategy ahead of Hannah's well-being? He literally needed to take the bull by the horns. Especially if he was that bull!

He took a deep breath. Tucked in his shirt. Ran a hand through his hair. Had a quick look in the mirror. Just like that teenage boy about to meet his crush.

"You're pathetic," he muttered to himself. Still, he felt like a warrior heading to battle as he marched down the hall.

He paused at the closed door of Hannah's room. He could hear them in there. Shelby was singing "Old MacDonald." She was at the pig part.

"With a—*snort snort*—here…" No wonder Hannah was laughing!

Did he knock? It was *his* house! He took a deep breath, and opened the door. They were on Hannah's bed, Shelby sitting cross-legged on the edge of it, and Hannah kneeling behind her.

Hannah was braiding Shelby's hair.

They were both in their pajamas. There was nothing remotely sexy about Shelby's attire, pink cotton drawstring pants, and a tank top not unlike the one she had worn the other day in the sprinkler. Except maybe this one was a little thinner.

If she got wet in that top, he was pretty sure he wouldn't see a bra underneath it. It was obvious she didn't have on any underwear.

The teenage boy in him clamored.

"Here an *oink*, there an *oink*, everywhere an *oink-oink*—" She suddenly realized they were no longer alone. She stopped, turned her head to look at him, and blushed.

Her hair was falling out of the clumsy braid, curling around the sun-kissed delicacy of her face. He'd forgotten—or had been trying to forget—those eyes. Brown, but so generously flecked with green and gold that just to say brown seemed like a crime of inadequate use of the language.

He saw, despite the laughter, the depth in her, layers. And shadows, too.

"Don't stop for me," he said, and hoped his voice

wasn't a tiny bit hoarse, though he was sure it was. "That's a mighty fine *oink* you got there."

He swore to himself. Of all the things he could have said, had he just told Shelby Kane that she did a mighty fine *oink*?

He told the clamoring inner boy that it was just as he had been telling himself all week.

Shelby Kane was like a big kid.

The inner teen wasn't buying it.

"Isn't it?" Hannah said. "Daddy, you should hear her do a duck. Shelby, do your duck for Daddy."

"Um, not right now," she said, embarrassed.

"Daddy. Come look at what I'm doing."

I can see from here, thank you. No sense letting Shelby know what she was doing to him. He walked over.

"Very nice," he said, with what he hoped was zero inflection.

"Do you want to try?" Hannah asked.

"No!" There was some inflection in that!

"But you could learn how to do mine," Hannah said.

He didn't have any desire to learn how to do hers. Did that make him a bad dad? If he changed his mind, that's what the internet was for.

"I had a text from the McKinnons," he said, changing the topic, even as he could imagine his hands in Shelby's hair. "Do you want to go over there tomorrow and play with Crystal?"

"Yes!" Hannah squealed. And then her face

crumpled and she slid a look at Shelby's back. "Oh. Maybe not."

Even not seeing Hannah's face, Sam understood instantly his daughter was trying not to hurt Shelby's feelings by choosing a different playmate. Sometimes, he felt as if—hair braiding aside—maybe he was doing something right in the daddy department.

"Hannah, I want you to go!" Shelby said. "It would be perfect if you did. I need to go shopping for a few things. I'm getting tired of rinsing my—"

She stopped. Her blush deepened.

There was something so appealing about this young woman, daughter of one of the richest people in the world, having no masks.

"You need a bathing suit!" Hannah said.

Apparently her need of a bathing suit was right up there with the unmentionables hanging over her bathroom shower rod.

"I think I need some pants that fit better."

"No, you *need* a bathing suit," Hannah said officiously. "Because we play in the sprinkler every day."

"All right," Shelby said. "I'll see if I can find a bathing suit."

"Do you like one-piece or two-pieces?" Hannah asked.

Lord have mercy, Sam thought.

Shelby seemed to consider, tilting her head

thoughtfully. Did she cast him a quick glance? "I think for the sprinkler, one-piece."

See? The occasional prayer was answered. If word got around that Shelby was cavorting through the sprinkler in a bikini, he probably wouldn't be able to stop a full-fledged stampede up from the barn in the heat of the day.

"And what about on the beach?" Hannah asked.

"You're not going to the beach anytime soon," he snapped.

Hannah gave him a *what's up with you?* look.

"But if we did," Hannah insisted.

This time it was Shelby, not the good Lord, who showed him mercy. "Let's not worry about that right now. I'll go to the nearest town tomorrow and see what I can find."

He could not help but appreciate how she had so quickly and skillfully allowed Hannah to do what she wanted, without feeling guilty about her choice.

"You'll come back?" Hannah asked, and he made note of that. Was his daughter already attached? Worried about loss? Had a temporary arrangement with Shelby been a mistake? Was he reading too much into it? Way too much?

"Of course I'm coming back!"

Hannah visibly relaxed. So did he. Only he hoped not visibly.

"Where is the nearest town for shopping?"

Shelby asked him. "I know I came through a couple on my way here."

He suspected the little towns she had passed on her way here would have a good selection of work boots, plaid shirts, and farm and ranch supplies. No bathing suits.

Another thought occurred to him.

Don't do it, he ordered himself.

Be a better man, another part of him insisted.

She had made his daughter happy. It was one thing to avoid her, it was another not to let her know how much he appreciated her.

"Um, I'll be taking the ranch helicopter to drop off Hannah and then to continue to Calgary. Why don't you come with us?" Well, *us* for part of the way. He and she alone, for the rest of it.

For Pete's sake! He'd be piloting a helicopter, an activity he thoroughly enjoyed because it required such intensity of focus. And not on her hair, either!

When Shelby didn't answer right away, he felt compelled to convince her.

Because he owed her for his daughter's happiness.

The teenage boy inside him snickered.

"It'll save you a couple of hours of driving on lonely roads."

He wondered if she might be feeling as awkward about spending time with him as he was with her. Had the avoidance been working two ways? For some reason that hurt in the same way that Hannah not appearing to miss him had hurt.

"I'll be in meetings, so you'll be free to shop to your heart's content. You should get a dress for the grad."

"The grad?" she said, surprised. "I'm invited to that?"

"Of course, silly," Hannah said, "*Everybody* goes."

"It's a really small high school," Sam said. "We only have seven grads this year. But Hannah's right. *Everyone* comes. Grandparents, aunts and uncles, cousins, babies. This year they've called it *Taking on the World!* It's kind of *the* event around here."

Why was he suddenly invested in her attending? He didn't want her to know that.

"I thought it might interest you," he said. "You know. Professionally. To see how a small, rural community holds an event. They always do a pretty amazing job."

"I *do* enjoy seeing how other events are put together. What kind of dress would I need?"

Which meant she was going to say yes, didn't it? He didn't quite know how to respond to that. How many kinds of dresses were there?

"A nice one," Hannah supplied.

"That's helpful. Calgary it is," Shelby said with a tentative smile.

What the hell was he doing?

"We'll leave around nine tomorrow morning."

"Sounds great."

Did it?

"Good night, Hannah-Banana," he said hastily to his daughter, and forewent his nightly hug in favor of getting out of that room as quickly as he could.

Shelby had done her best to freshen up the slack suit she had arrived in, but the truth was she was deliriously happy to be going shopping. She was sick to death of the nightly washing of undies, rolled jeans and ill-fitting tops.

She was sick to death of not being noticed by Sam Waters.

She felt ridiculously obsessed with him, straining her eyes to catch glimpses of him in the distance, straining her ears to hear him come in the house, feeling her heart start to pound hoping he would join them.

Playing in the sprinkler.

Or for a good night story.

But, since that afternoon in the sprinkler Sam Waters had become as elusive as a ghost.

But when she came down to breakfast she had to acknowledge her delirious happiness had so much less to do with fresh undies than it had to do with him.

CHAPTER ELEVEN

SAM WAS, for the first time since they had shared mouse pancakes, in the kitchen when she arrived.

His preference for dress seemed to be business casual, and often with a Western flair, like a suit accompanied with boots and a cowboy hat, but this morning Sam was in full businessman mode. And he looked every inch the billionaire that he was.

"You've had a haircut," she said. Maybe she should have pretended she hadn't noticed. But how could she not notice that? And how was it, even without those curls, she still wanted to run her fingers through his hair? Just to see if it felt as silky as it looked.

"Yeah, Buckie took the shears to me. Does it look okay?"

"Fine," she bit out, instead of saying, *of course it looks okay. Better than okay! Sam Waters, you look ready for your GQ cover shoot.*

She really was not sure which look she liked best on him. This morning, the cowboy had been banished. As well as the business-ready haircut, Sam was freshly clean-shaven. In the same way his hair begged for her touch, that shaved skin made her want to put her fingertips on the tenderness of it.

Sam was sharply dressed in a pale gray suit. Shelby could tell from the way it fit him to absolute perfection—the jacket hugging the broadness of his shoulders, the pants skimming the large muscles of his thighs—that it was custommade by a really exquisite tailor. With it he had on a crisp white linen shirt and a black silk tie. The knife-pressed pants finished with a polished black dress shoe.

"Dresses up pretty good, huh?" Alvin said, coming into the kitchen. Shelby blushed that she had been caught staring, and wished she was not in a suit that was still crumpled despite her efforts to steam it in the bathroom beside the shower.

She was happy for the distraction of getting Hannah ready to go, but then they were all in the helicopter, and Sam was piloting.

"You fly?" she asked, as he settled Hannah in the back and directed her to the seat beside him.

"The pilot called in sick. I thought I'd give it a whirl."

Shelby realized he was teasing her, like he had about her mistaking a bear for a dog, way back on day one. Why did that already feel as if it belonged in a different lifetime?

The tiny intimacy of his teasing sent a tickle up her spine. She adjusted her headset and gave in to the temptation to tease him back.

"You know, you could do a whole beefcake calendar by yourself. Cowboy. Businessman. Pilot."

Pilot was *very* attractive, the headset, the mirrored aviator glasses, his calm and confidence as he began to flick switches.

"What's a beefcake calendar?" Hannah asked innocently through her own headset.

He looked up from his control panel and raised an eyebrow at Shelby, mocking her knowledge of such things without saying a word.

"Oh, it's a calendar with a picture of a cute guy for every month of the year. They represent different jobs, like a fireman and a policeman," Shelby choked out. She wished she could take that back and omit the cute part.

"I might be a police when I grow up," Hannah said. Then she leaned forward in her seat, and regarded her father solemnly. "He's not cute," she decided. "He's my dad."

"Hey!' he said, mock-offended. "Dads can be cute."

Can they ever, Hannah thought.

Then, thankfully, the blades began to spin, slowly and then faster and faster, until the helicopter lifted off the ground. The takeoff took the focus off of cute dads, though Sam's competence at the controls of the helicopter was at least as appealing as his cuteness and the way he was rocking that suit!

Shelby, totally aware that the broadness of that shoulder nearly touching hers was adding to the exquisiteness of the experience, took in the absolute beauty of the country they were flying over.

Sam pointed out the boundaries of the huge ranch and—she was fairly certain—deliberately detoured to allow her to see more of it. There were forests and meadows, herds of fat cattle, a pasture of horses, the meandering creek, a spectacular waterfall.

They landed briefly at a neighboring ranch and off-loaded Hannah, who was excited to see her friend Crystal. She waved goodbye and then never glanced back.

And now they were alone.

"You're really good with Hannah," Sam said. He was piloting the aircraft with the casual confidence with which most men would handle a car. She liked the way his voice sounded coming through the headset. Raspy. Close.

"I just love hanging out with her." In fact, she was already wondering about the hole that was going to be left in her life when her ten days here were up.

There were only five days left. She was counting. How had five whole days gone by in such a flash?

"Your mom must have been terrific."

The question caught her totally off guard. "I don't know if she was or not."

He gave her a quizzical look.

And she said something she had never said to anyone before. "I don't remember my mom."

"What? You don't?"

"Do you think that's strange?" she asked. Why was she asking him this? Was it too personal?

Maybe there was something about having your life, literally, in the hands of someone that inspired trust. "I mean, I was ten. You'd think I'd remember something. But I don't."

He glanced at her. "You were probably traumatized by her death. I think people handle trauma in different ways. I try to make sure Hannah knows who her mom was. As painful as it is, I go through the baby albums with her, and tell her stories about things Beth and I did together, the things we did for that short time that we were allowed to be a family."

Something shivered along Shelby's spine. Why hadn't her father ever done anything like that? She recalled, with sudden intensity, feeling very alone with her pain after her mother's accident.

She frowned.

"What's wrong?" he asked softly, glancing at her, and then returning his attention to piloting.

"I just… I don't remember my dad ever doing anything like that. I have photos of my mom, but I don't recall us ever looking at them together. In

fact…" She went silent. She did remember something, after all.

"In fact?" he prodded her.

"In fact, I think my dad may have been relieved."

He was silent for a moment, and then he looked
at her with a look so authentically caring that it
felt as if it could melt a place in her she had not
been aware was frozen, until just this moment.

"I'm sorry," he said.

Shelby's memories of that time in her life felt
as if they were shrouded in fog, and that one
thing—her father's relief—had poked through
for a startling moment. Though she had a few
photos of her mom, hadn't other traces of her
disappeared from their lives with rather astound-
ing rapidness?

Or was that memory playing tricks on her? No
wonder she didn't recall that time of her life! It
was painful and confusing.

But somehow, being part of a household had
made her realize her aversion to commitment,
her reluctance to have children, were related to
the things she could not remember.

She couldn't remember? Or she didn't want to?

"Are you okay?" Sam asked.

Again, there was something in his voice that
made her want to lean into whatever he was offering.

Strength. Trustworthiness. The comfort of a
shared burden.

But she didn't lean into it. She leaned away from it.

"Yes, of course," Shelby told Sam, her tone deliberately breezy. "I'm fine. How could I not be? What a spectacular day."

Even though his eyes were hidden by the sexy sunglasses, his expression was dubious, as if he saw right through her, to something she had never even allowed herself to see.

The pain was still there. Right below the surface. It had probably controlled almost every single decision about her whole life.

But she was not going to let it spoil today!

"You're a good dad," she told him, anxious to take the focus off herself and avoid this feeling of weakness, as if she wanted to share deep confidences with him.

He smiled, something a little weary in the expression. "Some days are better than others," he said. "Parenting a little girl, particularly alone, feels as if I'm navigating a minefield. When I get through another day without a catastrophe, I feel euphoric."

"What kind of catastrophe?" Shelby asked.

"Let's see, the no ice cream for supper one, the bath one, the bedtime one, the hair one—especially the hair one…"

"But I haven't seen any of that."

"That's why I thought you must have had a really good mom. Because you're so natural at it."

A natural mommy? Her? The one who had never wanted to have children? The one who, when women her age started talking about having children, felt terrified?

"She's done really well since you came," Sam continued. "No tantrums. No pointing her dolls at anyone in a threatening manner. Tamed hair."

"Hannah is confident and creative, empathetic and fun. That's all the proof you need that you are doing so much right."

"Well, maybe it's Buckie," he said.

And they both laughed. But he wasn't as distracted as she hoped he would be.

"Was your dad a good dad?" he asked softly.

She thought about that. "I think he tried a little too hard to make it up to me that I didn't have a mom. I was overindulged."

"All the more impressive that you've started your own business."

"Thank you. Given that I was basically raised to believe I was a princess, I think I've managed to shock quite a few people by being hardworking and practical and quite good at what I do. My dad didn't understand that people need a purpose. My business gave me one."

And so, she thought, did being with Hannah. And Sam.

"And, you know, my dad did his best. I see that more now than I ever did. Even though he was clumsy about loving a child, I always felt as if he had my back. Even when I was bratty."

"You, bratty?" He had that teasing tone again, and she liked it. Again, she could feel herself, emotionally, leaning into him.

"I acted like I was thirteen until I was about twenty-three."

"In terms of Hannah, I'm scared of what thirteen is going to look like."

"And well you should be."

"Particularly if it lasts ten years!" he said with mock panic.

They both chuckled over that.

"Anyway, that's why Boswell's birthday party is so important to me. To let him know how much I appreciate him doing a job alone that usually takes two... Just like you," she finished softly.

He gave her a look of gratitude. The moment passed, and yet it felt as if they had shared something important, a trust springing up between them.

They landed and Sam had a car and a driver waiting at the small airport on the outskirts of Calgary. They sat side by side in the luxurious back seat, leaning close as he used his phone and showed her some of the downtown shopping areas. They exchanged phone numbers so they could arrange to meet when his meeting was over.

The car pulled over to drop her off. Sam got out

before the driver could, and held open the door for her.

The noise and bustle of downtown Calgary was a bit of a shock after the quiet of the ranch, and he read her expression.

"You'll be okay exploring on your own?" he asked. Again, she was taken with his ease in reading her, his very genuine concern, and his old-fashioned chivalry.

"Of course," she said. "I'm from New York!"

He reached into his pocket and handed her a credit card. "This is preloaded. Get whatever you need."

She tried to hand it back. "No—"

But he wouldn't take it. "Let me do it for you. I owe you one. For making Hannah happy."

"You don't owe me anything for that. We've done a trade and I'm more than happy with it."

"It would give me pleasure, really. And if you see something Hannah might like…"

"Alright," she said, and couldn't help but be pleased again at his chivalry and thoughtfulness, warmed by how his daughter was never far from his mind.

"My meeting won't be long. I'll let you know when it's over and we'll go for lunch. I have a special place I'd like to show you."

He had a special place he wanted to show her? What was taking shape between them? It felt frightening and wonderful at the same time. Or maybe she was reading too much into it. He was being hospitable. Maybe that was all.

Then Sam got back into the vehicle, and it slipped quietly back into traffic and was gone.

CHAPTER TWELVE

IT WAS A beautiful day and Shelby adored downtown Calgary with its wonderful combination of old historic buildings and innovative modern ones. There was a vitality about the city famous for its Western culture and its Stampede.

Though the Stampede was weeks away, she could feel the city gearing up for it. It seemed as if it would be an exciting time to be here, but she would be gone and it would be too early to come back to start on her father's party.

Gone.

Gone from Hannah. And Sam. And Buckie. And Rascal.

How could she feel faintly bereft over that? Probably just because she had been so intensely immersed in a world different from her own. It was only human that she would miss it. Though she knew, a week ago, if someone had told her she would miss playing nanny she would have scoffed.

It made her feel as if she didn't know herself, at all!

She gave herself over to discovering Calgary instead of indulging self-contemplation. Much of the downtown was connected by walkways, which functioned as protection against the many months of winter weather, though they were unnecessary today.

The shops and boutiques were world-class, and she gave herself over to the pure enjoyment of shopping. It had been a long time—since starting Eventually—that she'd had the time or inclination—or budget—to pamper herself. Despite Sam giving her the credit card, she used her own on everything, including the cutest little dress she found for Hannah.

When Sam called her, time had evaporated. Shelby had gotten all the essentials to get her through a few more days: underwear; socks; suitable shoes; shorts and tops; a pair of casual slacks, but she was no closer to picking out a dress for *Taking on the World.*

"Ready for lunch?" he asked. His voice over the phone was warm and sexy and felt like a touch on the back of her neck.

She looked at the sea of dresses she was surrounded by. "Hang on," she said. "I'm sending you a picture."

She took a photo of one of the dresses, on its hangar, and sent it. "Hannah said nice. What does that mean? Formal? Summer? Cocktail?"

"Hang on, it just came in."

Silence.

"Well?"

"It's a little, uh, I-hate-this-dress-but-I'm-still-hopeful bridesmaid," Sam said.

"That's a lot to tell about a dress. It sounds as if you've been to way too many weddings."

"Weddings are important in our part of the country. Community events. Right up there with grad nights."

She felt a tickle of longing for that kind of community. It made her feel the same way the first glimpse of his house had. As if there was a promise there. Of family. History. Stability. Tradition.

She ordered herself to focus and took a picture of the second dress. She pressed send and heard the ping of it arriving on his phone.

"Wasn't that in *Beauty and the Beast*?" he asked. "I think it's a bit too ball gown."

"Your areas of expertise are taking me by surprise."

"Spent the winter on a ranch with a five-year-old. There were at least a hundred viewings." He hummed the theme song.

She laughed. She snapped a picture and sent it. "Okay, this one."

"Definitely not."

Only this time, that sexy voice wasn't coming through her phone, it was practically in her ear. Sam was standing right beside her, looking at the dress.

"What the heck? How…"

"Magic," he said.

She stared at him. Her mouth had fallen open. She'd only left him a few hours ago, how could his pure presence be so newly shocking?

Maybe it was the contrast of all that masculinity in the distinctly feminine atmosphere of the dress boutique.

"M-Magic?" she stammered. Oh, yeah, she was definitely feeling that! "No, seriously, where did you come from?"

"I caught a glimpse of the shop tag inside the first dress you sent me a photo of. I was practically standing outside."

Something—pure delight—shivered along her spine that Sam was standing beside her, apparently game to help her pick a dress.

"I'm glad you clarified," she said, not wanting him to see how pleased she was by his presence, "otherwise it might have seemed as if you were a stalker."

He tilted his head at her. She was pretty sure she wasn't hiding anything from him. He was used to females plying him with unwanted attention. He'd said as much the first day they'd met.

Out of the corner of her eye, Shelby saw the three salesclerks exchange glances. One fanned herself and another pretended to swoon. Sam cast them an irritated glance, evidently well aware of his ability to cause a flutter in female hearts.

"Believe me," he said. "I'm not a stalker."

"Okay," she said, "I believe you." More like the stalkee!

"Thanks," he said dryly.

"This is the final of the three I've narrowed it down to," Shelby said, trying for an all-business tone. She held up the pale blue backless dress to him.

He looked at the dress for a long time. She saw his Adam's apple bob as he swallowed. "You'd steal the show in that one."

She felt like it was her turn to swoon, but she kept her tone light. "Taking on the world!" she reminded him.

"Maybe we should let the grad girls be the ones who steal the show."

"Oh! You're right." Again, his sensitivity impressed. Of course it was the grad girls' night to be the stars. But the fact that he understood that boded so well for Hannah's future.

"Something a little more subdued," she said.

"Mature," he agreed.

He turned to a rack beside him, skimmed through it, looked her up and down, and handed her two dresses.

"Try on these ones for me."

For him?

It was just an expression. Still, she gulped. She looked at the labels inside the dresses. Her size *exactly*.

"Excuse me, ma'am?" Sam called.

The salesladies, all three of them, rushed toward him. "Could you see what you have for shoes that would match those two dresses?"

They scurried off, eager to please. What kind of man thought of stuff like that? She realized Sam was not just a good daddy, he had been a fabulous husband. She felt a funny little ache in the region of her heart. Because her life had not had men like this in it? Because she had convinced herself that she was not the marriage type?

She put on the first dress, way too aware that Sam was only a few feet away from her on the other side of the door as she undressed. The dress was a beautiful butter-yellow cotton summer dress, button-down and short-sleeved, with a belt dividing the bodice from the wide skirt. She slipped on a pair of matching flats that had been put under the door for her.

She felt really shy when she stepped out to model it for him.

Sam cocked his head.

She did an experimental turn, and loved the way the dress swished around her legs, and how as she completed the turn, she saw his eyes resting there, heated, before he quickly masked it.

"It's nice," he said. "Really nice."

"But?"

"Maybe too, um, fifties housewife."

"Sexy fifties housewife," one of the salesladies chimed in.

Sexy? She thought maybe she should take it!

Or maybe not. It would not take much to push things into the danger zone between them. As if they weren't halfway there already.

Actually, hadn't they been flirting with the danger zone since that day they had chased each other through the sprinklers?

He knew it. That's why he'd been avoiding her ever since.

She tried on the other dress. Shelby had cut her teeth on beautiful clothing. She had closets stuffed with the designer duds she had collected, casually and carelessly, before she had chosen the path of poverty.

Okay, not exactly poverty, but not two-thousand-dollar dresses, either.

This dress was not two thousand dollars, not even close. And yet it held more pure enchantment than some of those very expensive dresses had.

The dress was a dark mossy green, fitted, with a dark under sheath and a layer of laser-cut lace, one shade lighter, on top. It was a nice length, ending just above her knee. Coupled with the matching high heels, it made her look extraordinarily, but subtly sensual, oozing feminine power and mystery.

She realized she looked very grown-up. And

she realized she wanted to live up to what that dress said she was. She realized she wanted to be the woman who looked back at her from the mirror, a woman who had come fully into herself, who knew exactly what she wanted, and knew how to get it.

What exactly did she want? Shelby was shocked by the immediate answer that blasted through her brain.

She wanted to taste Sam Water's lips. She'd wanted to taste them since the day they had negotiated the trade. And every day since.

Time was ticking. Loudly. She was pretty sure she could hear it. Sam would probably take up avoiding her again the second they got back to the ranch.

Something inside her felt as if she *had* to know the taste of him. Before it was over, in five short days, one of those days half-finished already.

Sam tried not to let his mouth drop open when Shelby emerged from the changeroom in the second dress he had picked for her.

On the hanger, it had looked lovely—exactly the kind of *nice* dress Hannah had suggested and not the kind—at all—that could make a man lose his mind, like that sexy blue number Shelby had shown him.

Maybe we should let the grad girls be the ones who steal the show, he'd said, and she'd fallen for it, never guessing how terrified he'd been to see her in that dress.

This dress had lied to him. On the hanger it had looked like something a woman might wear to tea at Buckingham Palace.

Off the hanger, subtly clinging to her soft curves, it was way worse than the overtly sexy one would have been.

Shelby looked simply, impossibly, stunning. Her eyes looked suddenly completely green, the hints of brown and gold gone. Why was he noticing her lips? They didn't have anything to do with the dress! She wasn't even wearing lipstick. Maybe, now that he looked, a hint of gloss...

Gone completely were any remnants of the playful child who played in the sprinkler and who could do great pig snorts. He felt as if the tomboyish girl in her borrowed clothes had transformed to a full-blooded woman before his very eyes.

"What do you think?" she asked him.

He was pretty sure she knew what he thought!

He hardly trusted himself to speak. He ordered himself to say, *sure, it will do.*

But he didn't say that. He breathed, "Beautiful."

The dress. The woman. The possibilities...

Some awareness of each other passed between them, shocking and intense. He broke his gaze first, deliberately looked away from her.

"Ready for lunch?" he asked. "I'm starving."

"Me, too," she said.

But for food?

Was her voice husky? Were those eyes, made smoky green by the color of the dress, fastened on his lips? Was she noticing his lips the same way he had noticed hers?

This was just wrong. He had to pull himself together while she went and changed. Hopefully, without that dress weaving some kind of spell around him, he could go back to the boss/nanny relationship.

But when she came out of the changeroom, she was wearing different clothes than what she'd been wearing this morning.

The rumpled business suit was gone.

And she certainly did not look like she was impersonating Huck Finn.

She was wearing slender-fitting navy blue slacks, and a white sleeveless top. While not as flattering as the green dress, now that he had seen her like that, *that* Shelby lingered like a shadow.

He could see what a beautiful, sensual, all-grown-up woman she was. This hunger he was feeling, he told himself sternly, had nothing to do with his goal of being a better man.

Shelby Kane was his daughter's nanny.

Not technically, a voice inside him insisted on crowing. She was kind of an un-nanny. The terms of their agreement were based on a trade.

He wasn't really her boss. She wasn't even an employee.

His guest, then.

His daughter's protector and caretaker. He thought of all of them running through the sprinkler. That moment had been almost as sizzling as the dress. Maybe more so.

But it cemented the fact that over the past few days, Shelby had quickly become his daughter's friend. He could not do anything to jeopardize that. These feelings Shelby was stirring up in him were explainable.

He'd been on his own for a long time. He had not even looked at another woman since Beth died. It felt disloyal to be doing it now.

Five days left.

Since he was relying on technicalities, all of a sudden, four and a half. She would leave right after *Taking on the World.*

Anybody could do anything for four and a half days. A person watching their weight could give up cookies. A person who shouldn't drink could give up booze.

He could fight off his base instincts for four and a half days. He could be a gentleman and a better man. He could be grateful for all she had done for his daughter. And he could show her that. And only that.

CHAPTER THIRTEEN

"LET'S GO FOR LUNCH," he said.

"Yes, let's. Are you going to show me Calgary's finest?"

"I am. But it's probably not what you're expecting."

She sighed and her eyes met his. "Nothing has been what I'm expecting."

She didn't say that as if it was a bad thing.

He made a call, and had his driver come and pick up her many packages and deliver them the lunch he had made arrangements for earlier. Then, insulated bag in hand, he walked with her to the Devonian Gardens. Calgary's indoor botanical garden was an absolute marvel, a one-hectare oasis in the heart of downtown. It was spectacular with its ponds and fountains, hundreds of plants and trees, butterflies flitting about.

"I'm in awe," she said, taking out her phone and snapping pictures. "I'm adding these to my dream file. This would be the best place for an event."

She tapped her lip thoughtfully. He wished she wouldn't do that.

"I'd like to do a Christmas party here. Can you imagine? The juxtaposition of snow falling on the glass roof and the tropical atmosphere inside?"

He found himself enjoying seeing her in the zone, her enthusiasm and professionalism residing side by side. Again, he was so aware she was not his daughter's playmate. Shelby Kane was all grown-up. Finally, she had enough pictures, and they found a quiet place to sit.

"This is utterly amazing," she said with a sigh of contentment.

He was pleased by her enjoyment. See? He could be the perfect host. To prove it, he opened the lunch container and handed her a box.

She flipped the lid and her eyes widened.

"I figured you've experienced just as many five-star meals as I have. I wanted you to taste the real Calgary."

"Oh, this looks so yummy! But did you have to pick such a messy lunch? This top is brand-new."

"I didn't want you to leave Calgary without sampling Ray's Ribs. Don't worry. They sent bibs."

Bibs! That should take the awareness factor down a notch or two.

But it didn't. He shook out the large plastic bibs, and then found himself leaning close to her to tie the strings at the back of her neck. His fingers grazed the delicate skin there. Her hair had a scent to it that reminded him of the world after rain. Clean. Pure. And something else...

And then she took the other bib from his fingers, leaned into him, and he felt her fingers on the back of his neck, trailing heat. He could, shockingly, imagine her lips tracing that same line.

He reared back from her. Beware of a woman who could make a bib sexy!

She took a rib out of the container, nibbled it, drew it into her mouth, and pulled the meat off the bone, then licked sauce from her fingertips.

And he had thought it would be hard to watch her eat an ice pop! What had he been thinking! Sandwiches would have been a safe choice.

He looked at her lips, and thought *maybe, maybe not*. Maybe nothing was going to be safe in his world ever again.

No, that wasn't right.

Four. And. A. Half. Days.

"Earth-shattering," she said with a contented sigh. "I wonder if Ray caters?"

Earth-shattering is what it had been when they had run through the sprinkler together. Earth-shattering is what she had been in that dress. Earth-shattering is what he felt leaning into her, tying the strings behind her neck. All of life, even the simplest of things, had become earth-shattering.

"Tell me about growing up on a ranch," she said.

Sam did not consider himself much of a talker, and so no one was more surprised than him about all he had to say.

About his mom and dad, and his first pony, and hard work and bad weather, and the utter magic of the Mountain Waters Ranch.

"Of course, just like those grads who can only think of taking on the world, and not the world they already have, I had no idea what I had while I had it. I wanted something else. I wanted bigger. And more exciting. And more choices."

She smiled. "That's the song of youth, isn't it? More, more, more?"

"It is. Anyway, I came to university here in Calgary, and given my outdoorsy, kind of rough-and-tumble upbringing, I had a surprising knack for tech. I loved it. I started writing code, which if you're good enough at, you can name your own price. Instead, I started my first company before I graduated, and it got me all the *more* that I craved, and then some.

"Within a few years, *I* was going places I would have never predicted. My business was exploding. I had employees, I had offices around the world, I was making the kind of money a ranch—even a really prosperous one—could never dream of making.

"And I loved it all. The new people, the worlds that opened to me, the adventures, the successes, the accomplishments.

"But after Beth and I got married, we started coming back to the ranch more. She loved it there. She helped me see it through fresh eyes."

It occurred to him that he was talking about his wife without pain. For the first time, he remembered their partnership with deep appreciation, not tinged with regret or anger or guilt or what-ifs.

"She loved all things family," he remembered softly, and there was a stab not of pain, but of longing.

Family.

He realized it was what he wanted for Hannah: huge family dinners, games around the dining table, weddings and anniversaries.

And at the same time, he wanted to protect her from the loss that inevitably came from all that. The very thing that should have been most solid in all the world—that should be every person's safe place—could be snatched from you in the blink of an eye.

Love, that by-product of family, had left him shattered and unsure of everything. Most of all his own ability to be in control when it really mattered.

"With Beth, I came home to the realization of what a special place Mountain Waters was. We both started juggling our commitments to spend more time at the ranch.

"I'm so glad of that now. My dad was diagnosed with cancer just before Hannah was born. We got time with him, with both my parents. They got to hold our baby. My dad died before Hannah's first birthday, my mom before her second. It think my mom literally died of a broken heart. And then, still reeling from those losses, we found out Beth was sick."

Shelby's hand had found its way to his arm. She'd done that once before, that morning in the barn when he had also talked about Beth.

It was this—as much as the laughter, as much as her subtle sexiness, as much as how good she was with his daughter—that was the most dangerous to his battered and bruised heart.

His strength and been tested, almost beyond what he could endure.

Sam was not ready for any other battles.

And he was not sure he ever would be.

Sam contemplated all the things he felt Shelby's touch held. It was as if her strength flowed into him, filling up a reservoir that had emptied.

There was a kinship in her touch. They had both known sorrow and somehow, he was sure neither of them knew exactly how, they had survived.

And, in those fingers resting on his arms, he felt maybe the worst thing of all.

Hope.

That the light would come on in the world

again. Isn't that what had been happening for the last five days?

The sun had risen in his and Hannah's dark world. His daughter was like a little plant that had survived the harshest of winters, poking strongly out of the ground, moving unerringly toward the sun, lifting her face to it.

"I see the ranch now," Sam said, "as the best place in the world to raise a child."

"To heal," Shelby said simply. And he felt entirely seen.

"Yes," he said, softly.

A quiet unfolded between them. It should have been comfortable, but an awareness of her zinged in him.

She took her hand off his arm. He missed it.

"I feel as if I have sauce from my hairline to my fingertips."

It was exactly the right moment to insert some levity, and he was grateful to her for it. Shelby lifted the bib and dabbed at her face.

"You missed some right—" He took his own bib, and touched the edge of her lip.

Something went very still between them. And it was not comfortable, at all.

He could feel his heart beating hard, as if it planned to leap out of his chest.

She leaned toward him. He had time to move, but he didn't. He felt frozen. She reached up and mirrored what he had just done. She dabbed the corner of his lip with her napkin.

Her eyes were intent on his.

"Don't," he whispered.

"I have to," she said.

And then she kissed him.

Her kiss was light, the briefest touch of her lips to his. And yet it was a long, cool drink of water to a man dying of thirst. It was an oasis in a life that had become a desert.

"Why did you do that?" he asked. He hoped his tone was harsh. He missed the mark. It came out huskily.

"Just to say thank-you. For a perfect day. For telling your story to me. And inviting me into your space. And saying yes to letting me use the barn for my dad's birthday. And for helping me pick a dress. For these gardens. And the ribs.

"And most of all, for sharing your beautiful daughter."

A butterfly went by her, and she followed it with her eyes.

"Maybe," she said softly, "I'm not even thanking you, so much as life, and its unexpected gifts."

Well, they were his lips she had chosen to bestow her gratitude on.

But he understood perfectly what she was saying. They were alive. That kiss was part of acknowledging they were alive and that life—all of it, including the chemistry between a man and a woman—could be unexpectedly and breathtakingly beautiful.

And seductive, beckoning a person back toward the land of the living.

"We can't," he said, his voice a croak.

"Oh," she said, "I know that. Don't worry. I'm the woman least likely to want anything from you. I'm not the forever kind."

For some reason, instead of feeling relieved that she was not getting ready to post banns at the church because they had kissed, her words made him feel sad for her. His vow to keep her at a distance wavered. He could just accept the gifts of this moment. No, more than that. He felt *compelled* to accept them.

When her hand crept back into his, he let it stay. No, he closed his hand around hers, felt the perfect fit of their two hands together, felt all that softness against his own work-roughened palms.

He knew he was saying yes to the gift even though, underneath that bright wrapping, that gift might hide shards of glass waiting to embed themselves in his already tattered heart.

It was just for this moment. She had made that crystal clear.

The kiss had been a mistake. So why did it feel so good?

The truth was that mistakes often felt good, didn't they?

Tasting Sam had been everything she could have dreamed of. It had confirmed things about him, as if she had tasted his soul. It had told her that Sam was strong, but sensitive, practical, and extraordinarily deep.

The problem with a kiss like that was it triggered a longing for more. Shelby was determined to fight that longing, because *more* with Sam would not be the same as *more* had been with any other man she had ever been with.

She was aware she had chosen men who did not require much from her. He would not be that guy.

If Sam had been avoiding her before the trip to Calgary, it was her turn now to avoid him and all the complications he represented, and that the kiss had made all too apparent.

Thankfully, on Thursday, people began to arrive to get the barn ready for *Taking on the World*. It was a wonderful distraction from Shelby's awareness of Sam as she threw herself into what was truly a community event.

The whole high school seemed to show up, not just the graduating class. And with them came teachers and mothers, aunts and grandmothers. Fathers and grandfathers and uncles showed up for heavy lifting and ladder work, to wire electrics and to build props.

Shelby and Hannah were welcomed into the fold of activity. It felt like a beehive with so many people purposefully buzzing about. There were jobs for everyone. Hannah was soon engrossed in making tissue flowers while Shelby painted panel backdrops representing some of the countries of the world.

Over the next few days, the old barn was transformed into a global community. The grad committee had already done so much work doing props for their international theme.

Shelby suggested they set up the barn into zones: an outdoor area, comfortable places to sit and converse, a food and drink space, a game space, a place for the DJ, a place to dance, and lots of selfie zones. Shelby loved loaning her expertise to the group.

The grads set up a zone for each of their selected countries and themed it for that. So, you could have a quiet conversation in Paris, grab something to eat in Rome, have a game of beanbag toss in Los Angeles. You could dance the night away in Dubai, or go sit under the stars in Reykjavík.

Shelby's favourite was the selfie zones at the entrance to the barn. The first thing a guest saw was a huge papier–mâché globe that looked as if the students had spent most of the year constructing it and painting it. It was now suspended from the ceiling, and with the right setup, it looked as if the person in the picture was holding the whole world in their hands, literally *taking on the world.*

She loved all the prep for the big night, but most of all, Shelby loved how Sam and Hannah's community—their family—accepted her with open arms. She was totally embraced.

On Friday, Shelby and one of the grad girls, Sandra, were putting up the grad date on the wall in tissue flowers, threaded through with fairy lights. Tomorrow, the event they had all been working toward would welcome the entire community.

In a low undertone, Sandra confided, "I don't really want to take on the world."

"Oh?"

"I mean, most of the grad class wants to. They want to see a bigger world and explore new things."

Shelby remembered how Sam had told her he felt that way.

"I don't want to," Sandra said. "I don't want to leave here at all."

At that moment, Sam and the Mountain Waters Ranch hands came in. Under Alvin's supervision, two of them were carrying a huge vat of soup. Jimmy, his arm still in a cast, was juggling a tray of buns still steaming from the oven.

"I'll break your other one if you drop those," Alvin said.

If Shelby was not mistaken, Sandra's eyes followed Jimmy with an intense longing. Would Shelby have even recognized that kind of longing a week ago? She was pretty sure she was looking at Sam the same way. She hoped it wasn't as obvious, she hoped that maybe she only recognized that secret look because her heart recognized it.

"You know what I think?" Shelby said. "Most of the kids who leave will only know what they had once they don't have it anymore. Sam told me that's how he felt when he left and then came back."

"Really?"

"I think you have a special gift, Sandra. You already know what you have."

"But I don't know what to do! Not all ranches are helicopters and thousands of cattle and acres. Ours is a family operation, but my two older brothers already work with my dad. It can't support me, too. I live a long way from the nearest job opportunity."

Shelby contemplated that for a moment, and then a light bulb went off in her head.

"Maybe you don't," Shelby said with sudden inspiration. "Sam needs someone to help with Hannah. He hasn't been able to get a nanny who will stay."

"That would be my absolute dream job," Sandra breathed. "And I just love Hannah. Do you think he'd consider me? Really?"

"You won't know until you ask," Shelby said gently, but she already knew that she was standing with her replacement.

Soon Sam and Hannah would not need her anymore.

And she knew she was as uncertain about the future as Sandra was.

There had been so much activity and so much anticipation that it had almost made Shelby forget that after the Saturday night event, she would be leaving.

She had twin terrors warring within her. One, that her feelings for Sam had reached a dead end, and two, that they hadn't. Was it over, or was there a future?

A future? She was the woman who could be counted on not to burden people with claims on their futures!

One possibility made her feel despondent, and one frightened. She had a terrible history with relationships. Why would a relationship with Sam break the pattern? No, it would be best if she got off the Mountain Waters Ranch without encouraging any more complications.

CHAPTER FOURTEEN

BUT NOW SHELBY had allowed the forbidden thought: *a relationship with Sam*. As might be expected of a forbidden thought, it caused Shelby to tremble, and not entirely with fear, either.

Still, Shelby refused to spoil her final moments on the ranch by contemplating a world without Sam and Hannah.

She had to break the spell she was under. That she *belonged*. Because wasn't hope the most dangerous thing of all?

She frowned at that thought. When had that core belief formed? That hope was dangerous.

Shelby felt her younger self trying to whisper to her.

She shrugged it off. She knew she and Sam were both suppressing an electric attraction. That kiss had told her that.

But since then, she felt how his eyes lingered on her. She wondered if he could see the pulse in her neck pick up tempo every time he was around.

And yet, didn't they both know that following that sizzle could lead to disaster. Because then what?

It felt as if *Taking on the World* had become a pivotal point in her life, as if her whole world was never going to be the same, no matter what happened next.

So, when the event actually started, Shelby felt as giddy with fear and anticipation as any of those grads.

Hannah was also giddy with excitement, which was a lovely distraction. In her new dress she looked like a princess.

As they walked from the house to the barn, Sam and Shelby indulged in a rare moment of togetherness. Hannah insisted on taking her daddy's hand on one side and Shelby's on the other, and she kept leaping up, and they would swing her between them.

It was such a lovely, simple moment. Infused with that dangerous thing.

Hope.

That a future could look like this. Mommy and daddy and their little girl.

Shelby realized, stunned, why this evening felt so pivotal.

She had guarded herself against this exact thing her entire life, and yet here it was.

She longed for what she had experienced here on the ranch. She loved Hannah, and the little girl loved her.

But that made everything more complicated with Sam. A little girl could be badly hurt by a misstep between them.

She cast him a look out of the corner of her eye. He was gorgeous tonight, in a suit with an ever-so-subtle Western cut. He wore a black cowboy hat pulled low over his eyes and black boots.

What was going to happen between them? A fling? Leading where?

She ordered herself not to try and see the future, to put away the crystal ball, to just enjoy the moment and the evening they had all worked so hard toward.

They walked by the field that had been set aside for parking, which was packed with pickup trucks. Several parties had arrived by helicopter. Two planes had landed. Everyone from a hundred miles and beyond had come.

The grads—particularly the young women—shone like stars in the night. Their dresses were spectacular. Their hair and makeup perfect.

People mingled, enjoying the games and each other, laughing over selfies. Children, including Hannah and Crystal, darted in and out of the crowds, safe, watched over by their entire community.

The room hummed with an air of celebration.

"I'll go find us a drink," Sam said over the noise. "What would you like? A glass of wine?"

He said that as if they were together. She shivered at the thought of what being together with Sam would mean. It felt as if they were suddenly barreling toward an inevitable conclusion.

One thing she knew was that whatever happened tonight, she was not going to blame it on wine. And the fact that something was going to happen was popping in the air between them, like a downed power line snapping on the ground.

"Just water is fine."

He nodded and she watched him move away, appreciating his long lines and casual power, the way he stood out from the crowd.

He was waylaid long before he made it to the bar. It was Sandra, looking stunning in a mauve silk backless dress. She was looking up earnestly at Sam, and over the heads of the crowd, he sent Shelby an apologetic look, but she smiled and waved him off. She appreciated how he cocked his head, listening intently to Sandra, giving her his full attention.

Suddenly, they were both smiling, and Shelby guessed Sam had just found his perfect nanny.

He moved away from Sandra, but he was soon stopped by someone else. This time it was an elderly woman, and again he found Shelby's eyes, ever so subtly lifted one of those broad shoulders, before honoring that grandmother with his full and undivided attention.

She liked seeing him among his community. He was a man who could fit in anywhere in the entire world. He could walk with equal ease with kings and princes and probably had.

But it was obvious that he was fully in his element here.

She liked seeing how much this community loved him and respected him. She liked that almost everyone here had known him forever, since he was a little boy.

He was liked and loved for who he was, and that affection had not been caused—or corrupted—by his enormous success in the world.

It made Shelby's heart happy for Sam—and for Hannah—that they so obviously were in the place they belonged.

And where did she fit into all of this? She had never really felt as if she belonged anywhere in her life. There had never been a real sense of family or community. Could that change?

Even as she had longed for it, she wondered, did she really want it to?

Belonging involved commitment, the one thing she had consistently failed at her entire life.

Except for her business, and she was not sure that counted.

Shelby wondered if she had just been a temporary interloper in Sam and Hannah's world. If she was like a rock dropped into a pond and sank from sight, creating a temporary ripple that quickly disappeared.

But she forced herself to shake off all the troubling thoughts. This might be her last night ever on the Mountain Waters Ranch. There was no room for those kind of thoughts when the very air seemed to be infused with joy.

As she watched, Jimmy came in, his eyes searching the crowd.

And finding exactly who he was looking for.

He moved toward Sandra with a certainty that could make a person feel hopeful about the future and commitment and the whole world.

The music started and there was absolutely no moment of hesitation.

Suddenly the barn was hopping! Shelby lost sight of where Sam was.

"Could I have the first dance of the night?"

It was Alvin, looking very spiffy in a Western-style suit. He swept off a bonanza-sized hat and bowed to her.

"Of course!"

After that it was a complete whirlwind. She had always been popular, but at the back of her mind, Shelby might have wondered how much her popularity had to do with her last name.

Since it definitely wasn't that, she wasn't sure what it was tonight. Being the new gal in town? The amazing dress? Or was she, like Sandra, glowing with the soft light of someone open to possibilities?

Whatever it was, she just said *yes*. To every invitation and every new experience. One lovely older gentleman patiently taught her how to do the polka. She took part in the hysterically funny chicken dance. They danced the Hokey Pokey. The Bunny Hop was a fun-infused variation on a conga line.

Through it all, she waited for Sam to come and claim her.

But he did not.

And Shelby was not sure if she was relieved or irritated that her instinct that tonight would somehow be pivotal in her life was so off.

When had she begun to think she could trust her instincts?

Sam had long since given the bottle of chilled water he had finally managed to get for Shelby to someone else.

He couldn't get anywhere near her.

Which was maybe just as well.

At nine thirty or so, Hannah came and informed him, excitedly, that she had been invited to a sleepover at Crystal's. An hour later both sleepy, protesting girls had been packed into the neighboring ranch's truck.

So, he was not on daddy duty, and Shelby Kane was not his nanny anymore. Sandra Jefferson was going to take over on Monday.

Sandra's stepping up to the task was nothing less than heaven-sent, really.

And even though Shelby had never officially

been employed by Sam or the ranch, her position had kept a nice little barrier in place between them. As had Hannah's constant presence.

Now those barriers were teetering on the edge of total destruction, as he kept an eye on Shelby. They were lined up three deep to claim a dance with her.

It was nearing midnight, and Sam had not danced a single dance. But, boy, she had. Shelby was the belle of the ball. Well, in that dress, and with that radiance pouring out of her, it was little wonder.

Buckie was suddenly at his elbow. "Quit scowling," he said.

"I'm not scowling."

"Tell your forehead."

Even though he didn't want to admit Buckie was right, Sam deliberately tried to loosen up his facial muscles.

"Just go ask her to dance," Buckie said.

"Who?" he said, innocently.

Buckie snorted. "The night's nearly over. What are you waiting for?"

Maybe for the night to be over, for the moment to be gone, for the temptation to be successfully fought off. Tomorrow, she'd be gone.

"What are you afraid of?"

Sam wanted to tell Buckie he didn't want to wait in a lineup to dance with Shelby. He wanted to tell him he wasn't afraid of anything. But no words came out. Instead, he looked at the man, wordlessly.

"Oh," Buckie said, giving him a long look, as if he was a book, too easily read. He gave him a clap on the shoulder. "*That*. You're afraid of that."

Embarrassing to be so obvious.

"I remember the first time you fell off a pony," Buckie said quietly. "Come to your daddy bawling your eyes out. You remember?"

"Oh, yeah."

"He told you to get out there and get back on that horse, or he'd give you something to cry about."

"And there went his parent-of-the-year award," Sam said.

"I know folks do it differently now, but there were things to be said about the way it was done back then. Your daddy was teaching you to be a man. He was teaching you pain is temporary, but giving in to fear is forever."

"And yet if I ever talked to Hannah like that, you'd whup me up the side of my head," Sam pointed out.

"Huh. Well, the girl-children are an entirely different species," Buckie admitted. "She could help you with that."

He nodded toward where Shelby was bent over double with laughter, one of the final participants in a round of musical chairs.

As they watched, she shoved a man nearly

twice her size out of the way and plopped herself down in the last chair.

Everything was in that: her fire, her sense of herself, her strength. She was the girl-child who had been raised without a mother and still, despite it all, she had become this. A woman who could wear a dress like that, a woman who every man here recognized for what she was.

"You need to get back on the horse, Sam," Buckie said softly.

Sam didn't go ask her to dance right away. There was no sense letting Buckie think he was going to take relationship advice from a man who had never actually had one.

Except, he realized, he had. Buckie had had a relationship with this family for as long as Sam had been alive. He was rough around the edges, and yet, when it came to selflessness, he had always put the Waters family first.

Buckie was not just a cook, and certainly not just an employee. He was a friend.

No, a member of the family.

Like an annoying uncle.

Still, annoying or not, Buckie was coming from a place of having a genuine sense of being the family guardian. And unlike Sam, he was seeing clearly—very clearly—that there was something going on between Shelby and Sam.

It was time to find out.

What was between them.

It was time to find out if it was a one night thing, or if it was going somewhere.

Feeling like a warrior getting ready to stride into battle, Sam took a deep breath. He stepped out onto the dance floor. He pushed his way through a crush of people until, finally, he came to her.

He didn't have to say a word. His body language said it all. The men who had been clustered around her all night melted away.

Shelby looked at him as if she had been waiting, maybe her whole life, for this exact moment in time.

And he felt as if he had been, too. Nothing had ever felt quite so right as looking down at her flushed face and saying, "Could I have this dance?"

The music changed, just like that.

As if the whole universe had been waiting. For this. For this man and this woman to come together in this way.

It was a slow song, a love song. The mood in the room changed. The lights dimmed.

And when Shelby slid into his arms, and pressed against the length of him, it was as if she had been born to fit against him.

His hand found the small of her back. She tilted her head up to look at him. Her eyes were luminous.

"You're not my nanny, anymore," he said, his lips nearly on her ear.

"I told you from the start, I was never a nanny," she said, her voice husky.

But now it was official.

Just as he had thought, what was left of his barriers collapsed. He and Shelby stopped moving, leaning into each other, breathing hard. They stared at each other.

"I need some air," she said, her voice hoarse.

"Me, too."

CHAPTER FIFTEEN

SAM'S HAND ON the small of Shelby's back, he guided her through the crowd, avoiding that meeting of people's eyes that would lead to the stop, the inevitable conversation. He'd lost her once tonight that way, he didn't intend to do it again.

And then they were outside. He felt like they popped out, like a cork freed of a wine bottle. They were free of the noise and the crowd. They didn't pause in Reykjavík. In fact, in just a few steps they were swallowed by the cool, dark crispness of a star-filled night. Just yards away from that sea of noise and light and movement, they floated free.

It was incredibly hot for this time of year. He could feel a crackle in the air—a coming thunderstorm—that mirrored what was going on between him and Shelby.

And with the same suddenness that storm would start with, there was no preamble. She kissed him full on the lips, bracketed his face with her hands, took his mouth as if she was ravenous, her tongue exploring the curve of his lips, and the edge of his teeth, plundering the hollow.

"I thought you needed air," he muttered into the corner of her lips. He was shocked he was able to speak.

"I do," she said, her voice a husky caress that made his blood catch fire, "I'm dying. I need mouth-to-mouth."

"Who am I to turn my back on a dying woman?"

Her hands snaked under his shirt, leaving a trail of excruciating heat in the wake of her exploration. Her right leg slid up the side of his own. She pressed hard against him, so hard he could feel her pulse in her femoral artery.

"Come on," he growled in her ear, "we've got to get out of here."

He took her hand again and led her to the pathway behind the barn that snaked down into the ravine.

The woods were so thick the moonlight could not penetrate them. But he knew every inch of this trail. He did not need light to guide him.

Soon, the activity and noise of the grad celebration were completely gone. She kicked off her shoes and carried them in her hand, her bare feet padding quietly along the worn trail through the trees.

It reminded him of the first time he saw her, coming toward him, her shoes in her hand. He felt he had known, even then, it was leading to this.

He led her to a clearing, and finally they were free of the thick canopy of trees and had moonlight again. At this place, his boyhood favorite, the creek babbled happily into a pool. A large, flat rock overhung the pool.

When he laid her down on it, the rock was still warm from the heat of the day. There was an urgency about her, as if she could feel the coming storm, but he made them both slow it down.

He undressed her with reverence, the moon revealing her body to him, painting each perfect curve in silver and light.

They were caught in an enchantment, in a spell of meant-to-be.

Because there was no shyness in either of them.

But instead, a deep sense of recognition. Of moving toward what was always destined to be, something born of the same ancient rhythms and cycles that made rain and wind, dirt that grew things, and sun that warmed the earth so that they could grow after an endless winter.

They were in the grip of something, both of them, that could not be denied by something so puny as a man's strength or a woman's desire for a promise.

There was no yesterday. It—and its history, its memories, its lessons—had been completely obliterated by the sweet savagery of complete sensation.

As thunder growled in the distance, they explored, tasted, worshipped each other, explored some more. There was no place that was forbidden, there were no taboos.

Finally, they joined. They became the stars and the moon, the earth and the creek, the untamed storm approaching. Every barrier between them and the world dissolved as they moved in unison with the forces that had created it all.

When they were done, the tenderness he felt for her was overwhelming.

"It's not going anywhere," she told him, whispering the words against his neck as if they were a promise.

He was a man who had had his belief in forever shattered, and she was a woman who had never believed in it in the first place.

Could there be a more perfect match than that?

There were no more words between them, as if the place they had gone to was too immense for such a small thing as words to penetrate it, too sacred to try and capture its essence.

They slid into the pool, their skin so heated that the icy mountain runoff felt refreshing, as if it had been put there for the sole purpose of preventing an inferno, of cooling them off just enough to start all over again at the beginning.

The storm broke all around them just as they had finished making love for the second time. Shelby took in Sam, the beautiful cut of his muscles, the perfection of his skin. He was illuminated by the lightning flashes, before being plunged back into darkness.

The rawness of the storm was a perfect reflection of what had just transpired between them.

It was so *real,* so elemental, no frills or gadgets or flowers. No first-time awkwardness or discomfort.

Coming from a place of deep connection to all things, just like the storm.

The rain came, and Sam tugged her to his feet. Laughing, showering her with kisses, he somehow managed to get her back into the dress. He pulled on his now-soaked shirt, and she had to help him with the jeans which, wet, were sticking and gripping.

He took her hand, and with the rain sluicing down around them, the lightning splitting the sky, and the thunder rolling ominously, he led her along a path that followed the creek.

She was still barefoot—she had no idea what had become of her shoes—and the mud oozing up between her toes felt exquisite, her entire body so open to sensation, every cell celebrating it.

She realized they had skirted the barn completely and they came out of the woods behind the house. Despite the exertion of navigating a path turned to grease by rain, she was shaking uncontrollably.

They ran, hand in hand across the lawn, and up the front stairs.

"I can't get mud of Alvin's floors."

They both chuckled that such a rational thought was even possible. Without hesitation, Sam swept her into his arms, nudged the door open with his foot, kicked off his own boots without setting her down, and then carried her across the threshold and up the stairs.

It was so dark, but lightning flashes, illuminated the bedroom he had brought them to. It was beautiful, masculine, in muted grays with an impressive, solid four-poster bed dominating the space. But he went by the bed and into the en suite bathroom.

He flipped on the lights with his elbow and, peripherally, she noted the spa-like beauty of the bathroom: white towels, marble surfaces, a huge tub, a separate shower with multiple heads.

Sam set her down.

"Mud," she started to say, but he placed a single finger over her lips, regarding her with wonder, as if he had been deaf and returned to hearing to find himself in the midst of a symphony.

With simple masculine mastery, he stripped the sodden dress from her.

"Obviously ruined," he said with a touch of regret.

Worth it, she thought.

Sam reached around her and turned on the shower. Water poured like the rain outside from a showerhead in the ceiling, pulsed from a mounted wand, spouted out of wall jets. And then he stepped out of his own clothes, and they were in the shower, the hot water pounding them. He knelt at her feet, lifted them one at a time, directed the wand until the mud sluiced off them.

And then he rose, and as the water cascaded around them, he captured her lips once again, and they tasted each other, explored, and then tasted some more.

They stepped out of the shower and toweled each other dry. Then, Sam lifted Shelby again, carried her to his bed, set her down to pull back the covers. She slipped into the pure decadence of Egyptian cotton sheets and a down comforter.

He came in beside her. "What kind of man makes love to a woman for the first time on a rock?" he whispered against her. "I think I better make up for that."

And he did.

Shelby woke in the morning with a feeling like she had never had in her entire life. Entirely relaxed. Satiated.

Happy.

The storm of last night had passed, and sunshine danced in the large paned window of his bedroom. She turned to look at Sam, appreciating how the strong morning light spilled across the perfect male contours of his body.

He was laying on his belly, his broad back bare,

the comforter riding the line of two strong dimples right above the beautiful curve of his behind. One strong, tanned arm was splayed across her midriff, the other fell off the edge of the bed.

Sam's face, whisker-shadowed, was pressed into the pillow, and Shelby unabashedly, hungrily, studied the rumple of his hair. It was curling rebelliously at the tips even though it had been cut short. She took in the sweep of his lashes, the cut of his cheekbones and chin, the gorgeous curve of his lips.

As if he sensed he was being watched, he opened one eye, and then the other. He smiled at her with such tender and sleepy welcome she felt as if her bones were melting.

He put his hand on the back of her neck, pulled her into him, kissed her good morning. The kiss deepened.

"What about Buckie?" she whispered. "What's he going to say?"

"He has his own quarters, down by the bunkhouse. He has the day off today. It's Sunday. But it's not as if we're teenagers coming out of the hayloft all flushed with guilt and excitement."

"Well, maybe the excitement part."

"He wouldn't disapprove," Sam said, tracing the line of her cheek and her lips with a gentle finger. "In fact, he'll probably post banns at the church."

This was said casually, as if that would be quite all right with Sam.

For a flash, that familiar terror tried to rise. *Banns at the church?*

That sounded like a commitment. Is that where Sam thought this was going? She wondered what the future held, but then she decided there would be lots of time for thinking later. She had to go home today. She would think then.

Later, they were in his kitchen. She was wearing one of his button-up shirts. It had the subtle scent of laundry soap and him. It stopped just above her thigh, and it made her feel sexy and as if she was his. He was wearing the crazy boxer shorts that Hannah had lent her that first day in the sprinkler. It made him look sexy, and feel as if he was hers.

They made toast and smeared it with jam and fed it to each other.

"Don't go," Sam said, flicking a crumb off her lip with his finger. "Don't go today."

Don't go. What she feared and longed for.

"So tempting," she said, trying for a light tone. "If ever anyone was going to convince me to just throw the last two years of working and building a business to the wind, it would be you, but I can't. And I'm going to have to leave soon, within an hour or two. I've got to drive to Calgary and my flight goes to New York at three. And then I have to go to Mississippi for most of next week."

"Stay, just for today."

Just for today. Couldn't a person live their whole life like that?

"I'll get someone to take the car back," he promised. "I'll get the company jet to take you to New York tonight. You can sleep all the way."

He had stolen them a few more hours, and she was grateful for that. How easy it had been to forget, in the primal things that had happened between them, that he was *also* this. That he had companies and jets and a fortune at his command.

"That sounds wonderful," she said.

Several hours later, they took the helicopter and picked up Hannah. When they got back Sam saddled horses and Shelby took the opportunity to remind Hannah she was leaving.

"Don't go," Hannah cried, an exact replica of her father's words.

"I have to," Shelby said. "Remember I told you about the party I'm planning for that young woman in Mississippi?"

"I remember," Hannah said sullenly.

"I have to go do that. But I'll be coming back here, because we're going to have my dad's birthday party at the barn in September."

It occurred to her last night had felt as if she didn't need to think about the future, but because of her dad's party, their lives would be intertwined for a while longer.

They couldn't be lovers! What would it do to Hannah?

"Do you know Sandra?" Shelby asked Hannah, avoiding even looking at Sam, sure Hannah would read some change and some truth into the way she looked at Sam.

"'Course. She's so pretty. I thought her dress was the prettiest last night."

"So did I!" Shelby said.

"Jimmy's her boyfriend," Hannah announced.

"He is?" Sam said, his brow furrowed.

"Everybody knows that. She's a really good horseback rider, too. Daddy, remember when she won the barrel racing at the high school rodeo?"

"I do. Would you be okay with Sandra coming to spend time with you when Shelby goes?"

The word *nanny* was carefully avoided.

"Oh!" Hannah said. "Do you think she would teach me how to barrel race?"

And that was how easily Hannah moved on.

"Let's go for a picnic," Sam suggested.

Shelby knew she should say no. But she was not that strong. She would take these moments, even if they felt as if she was stealing them.

They took a simple sandwich lunch to the waterfall. The grass was still wet from the storm last night, and they spread a thick blanket over it.

While Hannah ran delirious circles chasing butterflies, they lay side by side, watching lazy clouds drift across the sky.

Hannah appeared and looked down at them.

"Are you going to be boyfriend and girlfriend now?" she asked solemnly.

Shelby shot him a look. He gazed back at her, and the understanding passed between them. This was their complication. It wasn't just about them.

Protecting Hannah had to be the priority.

"Grown-ups can be friends without being a boyfriend and a girlfriend," Shelby said carefully.

"How do you know about girlfriends and boyfriends?" Sam asked, not answering the question.

"I'm going to have a boyfriend, too."

"Really?" Sam said. He turned his head to Shelby and mouthed, *Over my dead body.*

"Shane Hardy," Hannah announced.

"He's twelve, for god's sake," Sam sputtered.

"I'll grow up a little bit, first."

"Would you?"

"He doesn't know yet." She cocked her head at her father. "When should I tell him?"

"When you're thirty."

"Oh. Really *old.*"

"Thanks," Sam said dryly.

And then a butterfly caught Hannah's attention and she was off, forgetting she had even asked that question.

CHAPTER SIXTEEN

"WHEN AM I going to see you again?" Sam asked, an hour later, as they stood at the airstrip.

"I don't know."

Shelby felt as if she didn't know anything. She needed time away from him. She couldn't think straight around him.

What was unfolding between them was terrifying.

Even now, her eyes kept drifting to his lips, and wanting him made her feel as if her restraint from throwing herself at him was an elastic band, stretching tighter and tighter, getting ready to snap.

She glanced at Hannah and felt her resolve firm.

She took a deep breath. "We can't," she whispered.

He looked at her steadily. "I know," he said.

"Don't call," she told him.

"I won't," he said.

His agreement felt as if it tore her in two. She got on the plane to Calgary. She did not look back.

An hour later, she was on the jet to New York,

in a supremely comfortable bed, thinking how unexpectedly she had arrived back at the life she'd been born to.

Only with such exquisite differences.

Sam was different from the kind of people she had grown up around. He was sophisticated, and yet that sophistication was layered with an authenticity, an awareness of his own power that money and station in life had not given him.

And she realized, gratefully, that she had that now, too. Since Eventually, she had come into herself in the most unexpected and lovely ways.

And all of it—the unexpected twists and turns of her life—felt as if it had conspired to bring her to this moment.

Where she was equal to a man like that, completely worthy of his love.

Worthy of love, a little voice taunted her. *Worthy of love.* It reminded her that Sam had not mentioned the word *love.*

And for some reason, she hoped he wouldn't, as if that could spoil everything.

Exactly one week from the day that she had become Sam's lover, Shelby was in the mansion in Mississippi putting together the final details for the debutante ball.

The house was beyond expectation. It had a ballroom, for heaven's sake, the wall-to-wall French doors thrown open to the evening breeze, letting in the scents of magnolia and honeysuckle and the sounds of crickets and cicadas, whip-poor-wills and nighthawks.

Everything was as perfect as she and Marcus and her crew had been able to make it, though at the last minute, she found out they were down two servers who had called in sick.

Still, every event had those kinds of glitches. She rarely felt this kind of tension over them.

Then Marcus said, "Ooh, la la, who is that?"

She turned and looked.

It couldn't be. But it was. Her world went from gray to color again.

"That's Sam," she told Marcus, trying desperately to keep her tone neutral.

"*That's* Sam Waters? No wonder you abandoned me for some ranch when we had all *this* to get done."

"I'm sorry. You have done an incredible job."

"Actually," Marcus said, suddenly serious, "I was only teasing. I've wanted, for a long time, to show you what I can do."

She made a note of that to herself: *let go of control.*

In the context of Sam's surprise arrival, she was not sure now was the time to contemplate letting go of control. Unfortunately, as she thought it, her eyes fastened on Sam, moving toward her, and she had a rather heated memory of letting go of control completely.

He was neither the cowboy nor the businessman tonight, dressed in slacks, a polo shirt and
loafers.

"Sam," she said. "What are you doing here?"

She ordered herself to stop being pleased that
he had remembered what the event was, that he
had gone to the trouble of tracking it down.

"Anything you tell me to do," he said simply,
his eyes drinking her in as if she was a long cool
drink of water and he was a man dying of thirst.

"The man with a private jet waiting will do
whatever needs doing?" she asked, trying to
hide her pleasure at seeing him behind a skeptical note.

He nodded earnestly. "You need dishes washed?
I'm your man. One of the debutantes drinks too
much punch, and throws up? I'll clean it."

For heaven's sake. That was almost better than
a declaration of love.

Love.

She could not let that word enter her mind. She
couldn't. That word was a temptation, a witch
holding out a poisoned apple.

It promised one thing and delivered another.

"What if the girls want a male dancer?" she
challenged him.

"At a debutante ball?" he choked.

Sam was blushing. She wanted to make him
blush. Lots.

"How's Hannah?" she asked, even though she

had FaceTimed her favorite little girl twice this week. She needed the barrier of his child between them. It was dangerous that Hannah wasn't here.

"She's great. I'll have to think of a great gift to bring her since I've abandoned her for the weekend. Though I'm not sure if she'll even notice I'm gone. Sandra couldn't be more perfect. Poor Rascal doesn't know what hit him. He's running the barrels half a dozen times a day. His tongue's hanging out so far, I had to warn Hannah not to let him step on it. They had plans to take in a local rodeo together this weekend."

"You can bring her back a Mississippi mud pie." She knew it would be a hit with Hannah.

"Don't get me thinking about mud," he warned her in a low voice.

She thought of him washing the mud from her feet a week ago.

"I promised to help," he said. "What can I do?"

"Well, um, I still have flowers in the sink…"

"Flowers?" Marcus huffed. "We're down servers."

"Or course he's not going to be a server," Shelby snapped. Marcus was taking this being in charge thing a little too far.

But Sam lifted a broad shoulder amicably. "Happy to do it. I think it sounds kind of fun, actually."

And just like that Marcus was hustling him off

to get changed into one of the tuxedos they had rented for all the waitstaff.

The evening was absolutely glorious. Was it because she kept catching glimpses of Sam that it felt as if it might have been one of her best events ever? He slipped into the role as if he'd been doing it his whole life, and she loved it that these young women had no idea their "server" was a billionaire who had arrived in a private jet.

It made her feel as if she knew a secret.

In fact, she couldn't look at him nearly as often as she wanted, because it made her remember all their secrets, and that made it very difficult to concentrate on work.

Finally, well past midnight, the last of the limos had pulled out ferrying the last of the debutantes and their guests.

Marcus handed her a box with leftover Mississippi mud pie from the evening snack and shooed her out, insisting he had it, winking toward Sam, and mouthing something extremely inappropriate.

She was going to insist on staying, but then she remembered the part about giving up control, and graciously accepted Marcus's offer to look after the wrap-up.

Sam had rented a four-wheel drive, and they rode with the top down through the muggy Southern heat. They came to a sleepy little town, the nearest one to the venue, where she had rented a hotel room.

It was not the kind of hotel room either of them was used to. When she opened the door the bed seemed like the only piece of furniture, beckoning them.

She tried for small talk.

"I can't believe how you handled being a server," she said. "I can't thank you enough."

"I'm exhausted," he said, giving her a mischievous grin that did not look exhausted at all.

"Oh, I think being waitstaff is way harder than people give it credit for."

"That part was a cinch. It was fending off Marcus and all those women that was the hard part. Hannah better not act like that when she's that age."

"Act like what?"

He emptied his pockets and dollar bills and little slips of paper fluttered out. She picked one up and looked at it.

It had the name Linda on it. The *I* was dotted with a heart. There was a phone number. She picked up another one. Different name. Bolder message.

"Good grief," she said, looking at the crumpled dollar bills scattered around him with the phone numbers. "They were tipping you? We have a strict no tip policy!"

"You forgot to tell me. I'm not sure I could have stopped them." He fished several dollars out from under his waistband, and then reached into the back of his shorts.

He was right. She could not have stopped these wealthy young women from letting them know they saw him, and wanted what they saw.

Everybody in the world saw that thing he had. That masculine potency, the pure confidence and power he carried himself with. He had it whether he was riding a horse, waiting tables or running a billion-dollar company.

And tonight, it belonged to her.

"Hey," he said, loosening the tie, "come here."

He pulled her into her arms and kissed her thoroughly.

"I have been wanting to do that all night," he growled.

"Me, too," she admitted.

"Ma'am," he breathed into her ear, in a slow, sensuous, bone-melting drawl, "what's your pleasure?"

He didn't wait for her to answer.

He decided *his* pleasure was eating Mississippi mud pie. Off of her body.

"You know what would make this perfect?" he asked her huskily.

It could be more perfect?

"A spray can of whipping cream."

After that, Sam and Shelby spoke often, both on the phone and video chat. They texted each other several times a day, little notes and jokes, the language of lovers.

Shelby realized Sam made her feel cherished, while not making her feel trapped or committed.

"I'd love you to experience the Calgary Stampede with Hannah and I," Sam said one night. "Will you come for a few days?"

Shelby drew in a deep breath. "What will we tell Hannah?"

"I've booked us a suite. Separate rooms. The Stampede experience will definitely be G-rated."

She was ashamed to admit, even to herself, she didn't know how she was going to keep her hands off of him. At the same time, she loved it that he was protecting his daughter, who had already lost way too much, from potential hurt.

At some level, Shelby thought, he *knew*. It was fun. It was beautiful. But he knew that it couldn't last. Shelby was not the right woman for him. Or for anyone, if her past history was any indication.

He had suffered as much loss as his daughter. He wasn't leaving himself open to more.

They were having a fling, pure and simple. They would not complicate things with promises they did not intend to keep.

Shelby should have been glad that they were so much on the same page. But, somehow, glad was not how she felt.

Instead, she felt as if she was facing a hard truth. She was not worthy of a man like Sam. She could not replace the perfect wife he had already had, the perfect mother Hannah had already had.

"So," she told herself, breezily, "the pressure is off. Just have fun."

But she was not so sure she had ever felt less like having fun in her entire life. Maybe it would be best if they called it off now.

And yet, she could not resist seeing him again. And Hannah. Why not indulge in the summer of love? Why not take every moment of happiness that was offered to her? A natural splitting point would be after her father's birthday party. Why cheat herself of moments with Sam before she had to?

The trick would be not to let Hannah see what was going on between them, to make sure the child was not in any way affected by the final goodbye.

When she arrived at the Calgary International Airport, thoughts of goodbye fled her like late snow melting into nothingness on a sidewalk.

Sam greeted her with that oh-so-familiar grin, a lovely platonic kiss on the cheek, and by putting a beautiful white cowboy hat on her head.

"This is the Calgary version of a lei," he explained.

Of all the things she had experienced in life, it seemed to Shelby nothing had ever been sweeter than Hannah's excited greeting. When she swung the little girl up into her arms, Hannah showed none of her father's restraint. Shelby was covered in kisses.

Even though saying goodbye to Sam was inevitable, did she ever have to say goodbye to Hannah? They could always write, and call. As long as the little girl wanted to.

She decided not to think about it anymore. She surrendered to the simple bliss of being with them.

Hannah and Sam were already Stampede-ready in plaid shirts, jeans, cowboy hats and boots. They fit right in with nearly every other person in the airport, though they were probably the only authentic ranchers in the crowd. Shelby felt slightly out of place in the slacks and top she had chosen to be subtly sexy.

Sam had booked a large three-bedroom suite for them in a downtown Calgary hotel. As they drove there, Hannah chattered away about Sandra and Rascal, Buckie and Jimmy, new calves and the possibility of a bigger horse for her barrel racing career.

The hotel was super posh, and the suite was over-the-top, even for Shelby who had grown up in surroundings like this. Sam showed her through to the master suite.

"You take this one. I'll take the smaller room beside Hannah's."

"Thank you." When he closed the door to give her time to freshen up, she saw he had laid out a

Western outfit for her. Just as that day they had shopped for dresses, he had guessed her size exactly.

She put on the jeans and plaid shirt, the new boots and the hat, then modeled the ensemble for her approving audience of two.

If she had thought she might feel foolish in her new "duds," as Hannah called them, she was dead wrong.

She would have been terribly out of place without them. The whole city had gone cowboy chic.

The hotel was at the very center of everything. Shelby quickly saw that Calgary, always vibrant, upped its ante for this ten-day Western extravaganza that always began the first Friday of July. It was called The Greatest Outdoor Show on Earth, and Shelby thought that might be an understatement.

She and Sam and Hannah gave themselves over to a whole city that was in party mode. They partook in street corner pancake breakfast served from chuck wagons, and danced on closed off streets. Shelby watched, open-mouthed, as Indigenous peoples in full regalia rode docile American paint horses through the middle of downtown.

By afternoon they had made their way to Stampede Park, where there were rodeo events, multiple concerts, and a midway full of rides, carnival food and attractions. Hannah rode on Sam's shoulders as they made their way through the throngs of people, trying rides and carnival foods that competed with each other to be the most bizarre. This year there were nearly sixty weird and wonderful offerings.

Sam, wisely, made Hannah stick to a traditional corn dog and some mini donuts. But at Shelby's challenge he gamely tried the ketchup and mustard ice cream, which they all took a lick of, and then they shared Shelby's spicy pickle lemonade.

As they laughed over the ice cream, Shelby saw people sending indulgent looks their way. They looked, she thought, like a family. She wasn't going to let the fact it wasn't true—and would never be true—spoil her experience. It was such an incredible day.

Sam had tickets for the chuck wagon races and evening show, but Hannah was worn out. In all that commotion, she fell asleep on her daddy's shoulder and so Sam and Shelby decided to return to their hotel. As they were exiting Stampede Park, he went over to a young couple, with a little boy, waiting in line to buy tickets. He gave them his.

It was such a nice thing to do. Shelby saw in that young couple's faces as they stared down at what were likely very expensive tickets and then looked back at him, the looks on their faces confirming what she already knew.

He was a good man, thoughtful and generous, in a world that needed so much more of both.

Back in their suite, Sam put Hannah in bed, came out and shut the door of her bedroom.

And then he took Shelby in his arms and kissed her until she was breathless.

"That couldn't have worked out any better," he said, not the least concerned about not using those tickets.

"I thought we weren't—"

"I thought we weren't, too, but Shelby, I'm just not that strong."

But he proved to her—twice—exactly how strong he was.

Later, they ordered food from another of Sam's favorite Calgary restaurants.

They made slow sweet love, again, behind the locked door of the master suite, in unison with the fireworks that ended each day of the Stampede.

CHAPTER SEVENTEEN

THE NEXT DAY, they took in a few morning acti-
vates geared to children, but opted to take the afternoon off so that Hannah wouldn't be too tired
for the evening show.

They played a board game in the hotel room.

After the sixth round, Sam said to Shelby, "I'm
so sorry I packed this. The little fiend is tortur-
ing us."

"I'm not a fiend!" Hannah said. "And I win
again."

Shelby did not think it was torture at all. She
loved the lazy feeling of whiling away a hot afternoon in the air-conditioned room with two people
she had come to adore.

What was she going to do when they were no
longer part of her life? She warned herself, again,
about spoiling what she had in the moment by
worrying about the future.

They made their way back to Stampede Park in
late afternoon. It was the last night of the chuck
wagon races for the Cowboys Rangeland Derby.

Sam had been invited by one of his neighbors, who owned and drove one of the chuck wagon outfits. This time they didn't need tickets. They wore passes on lanyards.

The barbecues and tables were set up just outside the stable area, right beside the track and underneath a grandstand reserved for families, friends, special guests and VIPs.

It was soon evident Sam fell into several of those categories, but probably mostly the friend one. He knew many of these people, and Shelby could see their respect for him and his for them.

The pre-race dinner reminded Shelby of the grad celebration that had been held in the Mountain Waters Ranch barn. Generations of families were hanging out here. Children, whom Hannah knew, and soon joined, were running in and out of the gathering of people.

The only difference was that in this barn, they were sharing it with actual horses. Shelby was taken under the wing of the chuck wagon driver's wife, who gave her an exclusive tour of the stall area. The horses were so friendly and gentle, putting their heads over the stall doors looking for a pat. Shelby was impressed with the extreme love and care lavished on the horse athletes that participated in this sport. It was evident the horses were considered members of these chuck wagon families.

After dinner, they took their place on the grandstand seats. The majority of the audience was sitting across the infield from them, in a covered grandstand that Sam told her was probably sold out for this final chuck wagon race of the Stampede, and that it could hold north of twenty-five thousand people.

"Have you been to a chuck wagon race before?" Sam asked her.

"I've never even heard of a chuck wagon race before."

"They're the best," Hannah said, with a contented sigh, leaving her seat and taking up on her daddy's lap instead. "If I don't become a barrel racer, I might be an outrider instead."

As the first heat of four wagons came out into the infield, Sam explained what was going on to Shelby. As well as competing for substantial prize money, the colorful canvases stretched over the ribs of each of the chuck wagons had been auctioned off to sponsor companies in exchange for advertising. The highest-winning bid this year had been for close to two hundred thousand dollars.

The first chuck wagon races had been held at the Stampede over a hundred years ago, and they were still a tribute to the tough, courageous kind of men and women who had tamed the West.

"The Rangeland Derby is the World Series of chuck wagon races."

Sam was so patient, intent on having her understand this sport that he had grown up with and that was part of his culture.

He was a good teacher. He told her each team consisted of a four-horse chuck wagon, a driver and four outriders.

"That means, in a few minutes, they'll be thirty-two horses running that track. At the starting horn, one outrider has to hold the lead horse steady, while the others throw on a barrel, a tent fly and posts in the back of the wagon. Then they'll all catapult onto their own horses and follow the wagon as he circles the barrels, and comes out on the track. The outriders are not allowed to cross the finish line before the wagon."

"I can't believe those are the same horses I was just petting!" she said.

The horses were practically breathing fire, fighting against the traces, prancing, lunging, wanting to go.

The teams were announced. The drivers seemed to all have cowboy names like Chance and Cody and Lane and Dallas.

And then the horn blew. Shelby could barely keep track, so much was going on. But by the end of the race she was up and cheering them on with twenty-five thousand other people, even though her heart was in her throat as the thirty-two horses thundered past the finish line. The wagons had come perilously close together. The outriders had been absolutely hell-bent.

She leaned into Sam's shoulder. It felt so easy to do that. So right. She relished the evening light, the dust rising from the arena, the touch of his shoulder, Hannah on his lap.

It felt like a perfect moment, and she felt as if she loved life with an intensity made so much more exquisite by the feeling of belonging she felt with Sam and Hannah, and by the fact she knew she could not have it forever.

"You have to promise me, you will never, ever allow Hannah to be an outrider," Shelby whispered to Sam after the third heat of the evening. "I've never seen such daredevils in my whole life."

He laughed. "Funny. I find that less dangerous than those girls gone wild at the debutante ball."

Sam, Shelby and Hannah had now established a routine for watching the races. For each heat, they would all pick their own wagon to cheer for. Shelby picked hers by the names on the canvases, Hannah by how pretty the horses were, and Sam through knowledge—usually quite extensive—of the outfit.

He won most often, but that didn't prevent Shelby and Hannah from screaming themselves hoarse, cheering on their chosen wagons for each heat. When Sam's friend came out for his heat, they all chose him. They cheered and jumped up and down and pounded each other's backs with excitement. Sam's friend came dead last, and it didn't alter their excitement one little bit.

When the chucks were over, as day turned to night, the huge stadium lights came on and grand-stand show began. The opening number could have put any of the best shows in Las Vegas to shame. But Hannah was worn-out from all the excitement. There was a brief period of crabbiness before she fell asleep on Sam. They, once again, walked back to their hotel with Sam carrying the sleeping child in his arms.

Shelby was not sure there was a sight in the world more lovely than that.

"Those people are death-defying," Shelby said, handing him a cold beer when he came out from tucking the sleeping child in her bed. "That may have been the most exciting thing I've ever experienced."

He set his beer down without even taking a sip.

He picked her up as easily as he had picked up Hannah and carried her to the master suite. He shut the door with his foot, set her on the bed.

"I'm going to take that as a challenge," he growled.

"You won that challenge pretty handily," Shelby told him later. They were wrapped up in the thick, white housecoats provided by the hotel, sitting on their balcony. Sam was finally getting around to that beer she had opened for him earlier.

As they watched, the final fireworks of the Calgary Stampede lit up the city sky in a spectacular fashion.

"You were pretty good yourself," he said, wagging his eyebrows at her and then turning his attention to watch a huge rocket whistle upward, upward, upward. And then it exploded, and the sparks of color cascaded down. And then each of the sparks of color exploded and more fiery color dotted the sky.

She gasped with delight, delight that was deepened when his hand found hers.

"At least that good," he said, and then softly, "but I want more."

"You're insatiable," she said, deliberately misunderstanding him.

"I didn't mean more of that. I meant more of us."

"Didn't we talk about this?" she said, trying for lightness. "The song of youth? More, more, more."

The thing was, she didn't want more.

She wanted everything to stay exactly the way it was, right this minute.

"I think we need to talk about the future," Sam said softly.

"Please, not yet," she whispered. In her experience nothing could spoil a relationship more quickly than that particular discussion.

It occurred to her she was usually the one who

spoiled it, too. Why? She had never been in a relationship like this one.

Why did it feel as if she was quite capable of sabotaging her own happiness?

Sam could not believe how quickly the summer was going by. He hadn't been sure how to follow up that amazing weekend at the Calgary Stampede, but then he'd been called to Switzerland for a business trip. Shelby had been able to join him in Bern.

He'd liked the three of them spending time together, but he liked this way, way better. He needed to protect his daughter as he and Shelby got to know each other more deeply.

As lovers.

As partners and equals.

And as friends. He hoped the discussion Shelby didn't want to have would finally happen.

This was new in his experience. Usually it was the woman who was pushing for a commitment. But Sam realized it was him who could not picture a future without her in it. He did not even want to try. And he knew it was time to do the honorable thing.

She had to feel the same way as he did.

Love.

He was not sure when that had entered the equation, only that he felt it truly and deeply. He was confident she did, too, though she had not said the words. Still, it was in the way she looked at him, and the way she touched him, and the way she expressed tenderness to him.

Neither of them had ever been to Bern before and the beautiful European city was about as opposite to Calgary as you could get.

Being with Shelby made him feel so awake to the world. Open to new experiences, willing to celebrate the incredible differences that existed on the same globe. Everything felt brand-new to him.

This time, they spent grown-up time enjoying the gorgeous views of the Aare River, strolling hand in hand on the covered walkways, and availing themselves to the many charms of the Old City.

And then, once, when he found himself alone, he wandered into a jewellery store, and he saw it immediately.

The ring he wanted her to have.

That night in their room overlooking the river, the lights of the city reflecting in its inky darkness, he whispered the words to her for the first time.

Or tried to.

"I lo—"

Her finger had touched his lips, stopping him from finishing. Instead, she had finished it. They said actions spoke louder than words, and yet somehow the fact she had not let him say those words kept the ring in his pocket, waiting for the perfect moment.

But somehow, the moment never presented itself.

And then the next time they met, Hannah joined them again, this time in Shelby's territory, New York City. It was truly wonderful to explore that city that he was pretty familiar with through the eyes of his child.

"When I grow up, I'm going to work in this toy shop," Hannah announced, hugging her new teddy bear.

"I thought you were going to be an outrider," Shelby reminded her.

Hannah looked momentarily deflated.

"So much to do, so little time," Sam teased her.

But then his daughter brightened. "Outriding—or maybe barrel racing—is only in the summer. I'll work here the rest of the time."

"Hard no to my daughter working in New York City," Sam said to Shelby in an undertone.

"I turned out okay."

He smiled at that. "So you did," he said and felt a familiar bolt of heat race through him. He had that ring in his pocket, but he realized he didn't want to ask her to marry him with Hannah there.

Once they were a family, there would be plenty of time for the three of them. But for this—for his proposal—it needed to be just him and her.

They juggled schedules and locations all summer, meeting as often as they could, and still the perfect time never presented itself, though every encounter just cemented his certainty that Shelby was the right one.

The perfect partner for him.

The perfect mother for Hannah.

Even when they couldn't meet, he loved the sound of her voice on the phone, loved the texts she sent, sometimes funny, sometimes serious, sometimes so naughty they made him blush.

Still, though she was generous with the love hearts in her texts, Shelby had not said she loved him.

And yet everything said she did.

He was so glad when she came back to the ranch as summer dwindled to start getting ready for her father's birthday party. It occurred to him that this is what he'd been waiting for.

The perfect opportunity.

For him to propose.

He'd had enough of acting like guilty teenagers, he'd had enough of pretending to Hannah nothing was going on. He'd had enough of protecting his daughter and himself from the potential of hurt. Is that how he wanted Hannah to live? Afraid of all the things that could possibly go wrong?

It was starting to feel as if he was having an illicit affair, and lying about it. Lying to his kid! It was not like the Santa Claus lie, either.

It was lying about love between a man and a woman. He did not want his daughter to ever feel love was something to be hidden.

And it was time to lead by example.

CHAPTER EIGHTEEN

SAM IMAGINED IT ALL. He would propose. Shelby would squeal her yes and declare, finally, her love for him.

He needed to play by all the rules. He needed to go by the book. As a father himself, he had to make it right. As old-fashioned as it was, Sam needed to ask Boswell Kane for the hand of his daughter.

Knowing that was the missing piece to his proposal, he was able to just relax and watch how seamlessly his and Shelby's worlds combined. He got to see all the behind-the-scenes work that went into an event, and how good she was at it.

The barn had undergone a cute transformation for the grad, but what Shelby did for her father's birthday elevated it to new heights.

She had briefly considered a Western theme for the party, but she had decided it could too easily become hokey. Instead, she had opted for a formal black-tie affair, and he watched as she transformed the barn to fit that vision.

As the day drew closer, Sam was aware of feeling increasingly nervous. He rarely got nervous.

But when he finally met Boswell Kane, he knew exactly why he was nervous.

This was the father of the woman he was sleeping with.

Shelby had, in such a short time, brought the light to a dark world.

Not just his world, but Hannah's.

He was startled to find the presence of her father made him a little ashamed that he had not done the right thing before now. For the longest time, he had allowed himself to believe that what was happening between him and Shelby was okay. Better than okay.

He had lost faith in forever. She had been the perfect woman because she didn't want it at all.

But it had all started to feel terribly off. Not right. As if he was not being true to himself by not offering his protection, his commitment, his life, to the woman he had come to love.

He avoided Shelby all night because he was sure if Boswell saw them together, he would see, very clearly, what was going on between them.

Finally, the opportunity he had been waiting for presented itself. Boswell slipped outside and Sam followed him.

It was a gorgeous night. Chillier than the grad night, fall already in the mountain air. The pool on the creek would be a good place to propose, even if there would be no swimming in the creek tonight.

He was glad it was dark. He was blushing thinking about it.

"Sam," Boswell greeted him.

"Sir," Sam replied.

"No, no, Boswell, please."

Not until after he'd asked his question.

"Unbelievable place you have here," Boswell said. "Like nothing I have ever experienced before."

"I'm glad you're enjoying it."

Boswell wanted to talk about business! He wasn't familiar with tech things and he probed Sam's expertise.

It occurred to Sam that he had done such a good job of avoiding Shelby tonight that her father had no idea what was going on between them.

"Uh, sir, I need to talk to you about something."

Boswell looked at him shrewdly. What was he expecting? A business proposal?

"Um, you might not be aware that Shelby and I are, um, dating. Seeing each other."

Boswell tilted his head, squinting at Sam. "My, my," he said, "are you the reason my daughter is blooming like an autumn rose?"

"Um, well, I certainly hope so, sir. I wanted to ask you…"

He suddenly wished he had thought about this more. Maybe looked up how you asked a father for his daughter's hand in marriage. Beth's dad had died when she was young. Of a cancer very similar to hers.

Genetic, the doctors had said.

And still Sam had not absolved himself. What could he have done differently? Was he really going to do this again?

Yes, he really was.

Sam had made million-dollar deals. He ran one of the biggest ranches in Alberta. He liked to think he *handled* whatever challenges were thrown at him.

But now he felt like a gauche boy.

"Yes?" Boswell asked, puzzled.

"I wanted to ask you if you'd be okay with me asking Shelby to be my wife."

Boswell ducked his head and didn't say anything for so long that Sam was afraid the answer was no.

He hadn't considered that possibility. At all. What would he do if Boswell said no?

But when Boswell lifted his head, Sam saw the reason that he had ducked it in the first place.

His eyes shone with tears.

"You could not give me a better birthday gift than this," he said softly. "Thank you for my daughter's happiness. I cannot wait to get to know you better, as my son."

* * *

It was 3:00 a.m. Shelby felt exhausted as the last of the limos had pulled out, the Mercedes-Benz bus was gone and only one jet remained on the tarmac.

Her father's.

Lydia came and took both Shelby's hands in her own.

"I cannot thank you enough. This has been one of the most memorable evenings of my life. I mean that, Shelby." She cast Boswell a look.

Shelby could not miss the pure love in that look. "I'll wait at the plane for you, Bosley."

Somehow Shelby actually *liked* the endearment now. She was glad he had Lydia. Love did that, she supposed, softened all the edges.

And yet she felt a little troubled by her love of Sam tonight. He had seemed off, preoccupied.

As if he was avoiding her.

Maybe he had read something into her inability to say the words *I love you.* She felt if she said those words, the enchantment would be broken, like the clock striking midnight at Cinderella's ball.

It was silly. It was superstitious. And yet she clung to that superstition as if it was a talisman protecting them all—her and Sam and Hannah—from a darkness that waited. To destroy all happiness.

She shivered. Where was this coming from?

Except for Sam ignoring her, the evening could not have been more perfect.

That was a pretty big *except*.

I wonder if it's over, she thought, and a terror that she had mostly managed to tame over the summer roared back to life.

Good things did not last.

She had always thought the end of summer—this event—would be a natural concluding point for her and Sam.

But now that it was actually here, she did not feel ready.

Her father took Shelby's elbow. "Let's sit outside for a minute."

They walked to a bench that had been set up to overlook the ravine.

"I've been to so many parties in my life, I've lost count, Shelby. But what you just did tonight? It transcended. What an extraordinary gift to give a father. Not just the party, but an opportunity to see who his child has become. Seeing you in your element, I am just bursting with pride."

"Thanks, Dad. It was my privilege to do it for you. I have to confess something. I overheard you and Lydia at Christmas two years ago. Plotting to cut me off."

He chuckled. "And you beat us to the punch. That's my girl."

She was twenty-eight years old, and she was his girl. She still loved his approval. It occurred to her she would always be his girl. There was something extraordinarily comforting in that. She laid her head on his shoulder, and he put his arm around her.

"I had already started my company when I overheard the two of you talking. But up until that point it had been kind of a cute little distraction. Hearing you and Lydia gave me the impetus to take it to the next level. It started as *I'll show you* and it became *I showed myself.* Who I could be. What I could do.

"I have to confess, this party started kind of the same way. I wanted you to be proud of me. I wanted you to see me at my best. It felt like a lot of pressure to succeed."

"You achieved all those things, in spades."

"But something else became much more important to me. I started to look at it differently. I still wanted to show you, but I wanted to show you something else. It became not all about me, but about you.

"How much I appreciated you," she said softly, "I wanted to thank you for being a single dad, and doing your best all the time."

She realized her acute appreciation of single dads had a great deal to do with Sam.

"I spoiled you," Boswell said.

"I know. But it wasn't spoiling, like *oh, I'll throw some money at her and get rid of her,* it was spoiling like *I love her so much, and I just want to make her happy.*"

"Thank you for seeing that. It means the world to me."

"We don't say that much, do we, Dad? I love you?"

He shivered. "I'm sorry. I have an aversion to it."

Ahh, the things families passed on.

Silence sat between them for a few minutes.

"Your man is a fine man, Shelby."

"Oh," she stammered, "I don't know about *my* man." Especially since he'd been avoiding her tonight.

"Well, you better figure it out, because he had *the* talk with me tonight."

"I hope not," she said, trying for lightness. Where was this sense of dread coming from? From Sam ignoring her, certainly, but it had deepened since Boswell said he had an aversion to saying I love you. "*The* talk is what you had with me when I was eleven."

"He's an honorable man," Boswell said, pleased.

She knew, with sudden clarity, what *the* talk was. Of course Sam would be bound by tradition. He had done the old-fashioned thing. He had asked her father for her hand.

Where was the excitement? Why didn't it chase away the dread she had been feeling since she noticed Sam avoiding her tonight?

"Dad," she said, and her voice sounded as if it was coming from far away, "why can't I remember Mom?"

Boswell shot Shelby an uncomfortable look. "It's been such a nice night," he said, uneasily. "I don't want to—"

"Tell me," she said. "Please."

His discomfort, his uneasiness was already telling her something. That feeling of dread, intensified, shivering up and down her spine.

Her father sighed, took his hand off her shoulder, and knit his hands in front of him between his knees, and studied them.

"She just wasn't there, Shelby. Maybe that's why you can't remember her."

"What do you mean, she wasn't there?" Shelby asked. She could hear a funny squeak in her voice.

"There was something wrong with her," Boswell said, his voice faraway, remembering. "I didn't realize it until it was too late."

"What do you mean there was something wrong with her?"

"Even before you, Shelby, there was something in her. Restless and wild. It wasn't your fault."

Her fault?

"That she wasn't like other new moms. She never wanted to hold you, she didn't want to spend time with you. At first, I thought it was depression. That depression women get—"

"Postpartum," Shelby said, woodenly.

"Except it never went away. And you were like a little puppy, so anxious for her affection and approval, going to her for it again and again, only to be swatted away.

"She didn't act as if she was married and had a baby. She went out all the time, she partied hard. I suspect there were other men. That's all she wanted. The rush, the attention, the altered state of mind."

Shelby felt as if the cold started at her feet and moved slowly up, freezing her one cell at a time.

Her mother had not loved her.

Had not seen any value in her.

She had not been worthy.

Hadn't she always known that? Isn't that why she had chosen to have shallow relationships, easily left behind, before they discovered the truth?

She was not worthy. Even her own mother had seen it.

"The night she died, we had a terrible row about it," Boswell said, his voice low and tortured. "I always wondered if you had heard it. I'm ashamed to say, I don't know how you couldn't have heard. I practically lifted the roof I was yelling so loud."

And suddenly, she did remember.

She was a little girl, sitting on the stairs, her face pressed through the rails, her dolly clutched to her.

"It was the Beachwood Canyon house," she said, recalling the ornate wrought iron of the handrail.

Her father shot her a surprised look. "Yes, it was."

She remembered his voice, the rage in it. *Why can't you just say it? Is it so hard? I love you? All she wants is a little bit of your time. All she wants is those words. I think she'd be happy with a pat on the head every now and then when you walked by.*

And isn't that exactly what Shelby had accepted in every relationship? Pats on the head, crumbs of affection, believing, somehow, that's all she deserved.

But now, she had broken all the rules that that little girl had made that night sitting on the stairs, that terrible night that her mother had died.

She had run down the stairs. *Mommy, I love you.*

The look on her mother's face. Pity. Disdain, maybe.

No, horror.

You're suffocating me, she screamed. Her mother had slammed out of the house, angry. Shelby remembered screaming after her, as if it would solve everything, as if it wasn't suffocating her at all:

I love you.

I love you.

I love you.

Until her father had told her, sternly, sensing hysteria, to stop it. And then, not fifteen minutes later, they had heard sirens and seen flames.

CHAPTER NINETEEN

AND SHELBY HAD KNOWN, to the core of her being, that her mother was gone.

She was *responsible* for the fact her mother and father had fought that night. It was her fault her mother had stormed out of the house, gotten in that car, taken one of the canyon twists way too fast, and sailed off the earth.

Those words *I love you* had chased her from the house and straight into the arms of doom.

"I don't know," Boswell said, softly, "if she'd been drinking that night, or if that's what she wanted all along. With the drugs and the parties and the men, and finally that. Just to escape."

A child's hungry love not enough to hold her, just one more bond she wanted to be free of.

"I'm sorry, sweetie. I should not have told you. It's not a good note to end such a spectacular night on."

Always he had done what he thought was right, protected her from the pain of the truth.

"It's okay," she said. "Really."

And it was, because every single cell of her, and particularly the ones around her heart were frozen solid.

"Are you going to New York tonight?" she asked. She felt as if she was floating above them, looking down. She could hardly believe that cool, composed voice was her own.

"Yes, a red-eye, for sure."

As if he was sitting in the economy seats, not able to sleep, and not stretched out in a white leather recliner that went all the way back, with a steward gently covering him with a blanket.

"I think I'll come with you," she said.

"What? Just leave?" Boswell cast a look at the mess left in the barn.

"Marcus is here. And…" She couldn't say his name. It might thaw the ice block around her heart. "The bunkhouse was offered for him and the staff. They'll look after it. They know what to do."

"B-b-but why? Is it because of what I just said?"

"No, of course not." She suddenly remembered what her mother sounded like, and it was exactly like that. That insincere falsetto, that high inflection as if something really exciting was about to happen.

That did not involve a needy child clinging to her, screaming at her desperately.

I love you.

"Don't you need to let Sam know?"

She took out her phone and wagged it at her father. "That's what we have these for. I was leaving tomorrow, anyway. It will be way more convenient to take the jet with you. I'll just go grab my bag and talk to Marcus for a minute."

Her father looked at her face and it seemed as if he wanted to say something else. But he didn't. He looked back at his hands.

She got up briskly and moved away.

She suddenly remembered that about her mother, too.

Always brisk. Always in a hurry. To get away.

That was part of Shelby. Half of her, actually. You couldn't deny it just because you didn't like it.

How could she do that to Hannah and Sam? It was only a matter of time until her defects became apparent, until she cracked.

Better, so much better, to leave now.

Thank goodness she had gotten wind of the proposal before it happened. How awful that would have been.

How nearly impossible it would have been to do the right thing.

To say no.

It was a near miss, really, for poor Sam and Hannah. He'd been about to pop the question! To the most unsuitable person in the whole world.

She felt a momentary stab of anger at Sam. Why hadn't he just left well enough alone? Why hadn't he just let them keep going the way they had been?

Why did everything have to change?

Sam woke up in the morning and reached for Shelby. Despite trying to keep things from Hannah, he had thought she would sneak into his room when she wrapped up at the barn.

Sneak.

He was so glad, that as of today, that part would be over. There would be no more sneaking.

Love needed to be celebrated. Announced. Not hidden away.

He was surprised to find the bed empty. She'd still been at the function when he'd left at one in the morning. He looked at her pillow, at her side of the bed. He realized she hadn't slept there at all.

For a moment he felt pure panic.

No, wait, breathe. It hadn't been a party in New York City where there might be a nefarious person waiting, watching for her to have a vulnerable moment.

And she had not been drinking at all. It was her father's party, but she had juggled expertly between being a family member and the complete professional that she was. While she'd socialized—she'd known most of her father's friends and associates since she was a child—she's also been making sure everything was perfect, doing all the hard work in the background that made the magic unfold with seeming effortlessness.

He was pretty sure she hadn't even noticed that he'd been avoiding her.

Sam picked up his phone from the bedside table and frowned. It was just after five in the morning. Had she curled up out there somewhere, exhausted? She wouldn't have gone down to the creek by herself, would she?

She was getting to know her way around the ranch, but it could still be a dangerous place, perched on the edge of the wilderness the way it was.

But then he saw he had a message and that it was from Shelby. His relief was instantaneous, until he tapped the text icon.

And then he didn't feel relieved at all.

Sorry. Something's come up. Had to leave unexpectedly. Caught a ride with Dad. Talk soon.

Strange. No *babe* or other term of endearment. No little red hearts. No smoochie emoji.

It was five in the morning. He couldn't call her. On the other hand, she was heading to New York. It was eight there.

He tapped her contact, listened to the phone ring and ring and ring. And then he listened to her voice mail.

He'd always liked hearing her voice on voice

mail when he'd called her in the past. But he didn't feel that way right now.

He'd had a big plan for today. Her father had given him his blessing. He had the ring. He'd had it for way too long. He'd been thinking of things to say for way too long. He *needed* to give it to her. He *needed* to ask her the question.

Questions, really.

Will you marry me?

Will you spend the rest of your life with me?

Will you be a mother to Hannah?

Will you have my children?

It wasn't happening.

Not today.

He scraped a hand though his hair and headed for the shower. He hoped the hot water would dissolve the feeling in the pit of his stomach.

Of what?

He'd felt this way only once before in his entire life. Sitting in that doctor's office with Beth.

Impending doom.

Shelby's idea of *talk soon* was to ignore his calls for three days, and then to finally phone, something weirdly breathless in her voice, as if she was hurrying to catch a train or something.

"Sam," she said, "I'm so sorry I haven't returned your calls. Emergency at work."

What kind of emergency did planning parties leave you open to? He managed, barely, not to say that.

He respected what she did. He respected how she did it. But an emergency so compelling she couldn't answer her phone for three days? He was skeptical.

"Look," she said, "I have to tell you something."

What was with her voice? It made him want to ask, *Who are you and what have you done with Shelby?*

"It's been a fantastic summer, really it has. But my work is suffering. It's all pretty intense."

"Intense?" he said, stunned.

"It's suffocating me."

"What the—" He said a word that men say on a ranch a lot. Buckie's word for the letter *F*. He had never said it to a woman before.

"Of course, I'll call Hannah. If it's okay with you."

For a minute she almost sounded like herself.

"I'll just kind of wean her off of me. I don't want to hurt her. I'd rather die than hurt her."

She didn't sound like a woman who was suffocating. She sounded like a woman who was suffering.

"We need to talk," he said, trying to be reasonable.

"I can't. I mean to Hannah. But—"

"But not to me," he said tersely.

"That's correct."

Like a schoolteacher telling him he'd gotten two plus two right.

Shelby Kane had just told him he was suffocating her, and he was practically begging her to talk about it?

No.

He would not beg her to love him back. He would not. But if he stayed on the phone, he might. So he didn't say one more word. He disconnected.

Buckie waited two weeks before he addressed it.

"What is wrong with you?" He managed to get his word for the letter *F* in that short sentence three times.

"Wrong with me? Nothing."

"Don't give me that." He put his word for the letter *S* at the end of the sentence. "You're acting like a bear with a sore bottom. You got three hands and a cook fixin' to quit if you keep it up."

He didn't say anything.

"What happened between you and Shelby?" Buckie asked.

"I don't know, okay?"

He said that with quite a bit more heat than he expected.

"Did you have a fight?"

"No! She just left, the night of her dad's party. She left and she didn't say goodbye and then she called a few days later and said it was all too intense." He might as well say all of it. "She said I was suffocating her."

"You're dumb as a stick," Buckie said, all sympathy of course.

"Well, maybe that factored into it."

"She's lying to you."

"Maybe she lied to me before and this is the truth."

"Dumb as a stick," Buckie said, with a sad shake of his head. "It wasn't too intense, and she's not suffocating."

"How do you know?"

"You know, I might look as dumb as you're acting, but I ain't. I know human nature, and I know who that girl is."

"Yeah," he said sarcastically. "I remember. You saw it in her eyes."

"I know you been hurt, Sam. I know you suffered more loss in a short period than a lot of men get in their lifetimes. But you can't let it control you. You go talk to her."

"I'm so angry I wouldn't know what to say."

"Say that," Buckie said. "Say what's real. In your heart. If she still won't have you after you've had your say, at least you know you gave it everything. You didn't just quit. We don't abide a quitter around here."

Sam glared at Buckie.

"I'm willing to bet dollars to donuts that girl is hurting something fierce. If you love her, as much as I think you do, you'll go find out what's hurting her so bad, and you'll bring her back from it.

"That's what love does. It risks it all. It puts the other person first. It can hurt like hell. But it's still the only thing that can save us."

Sam said nothing.

"I need your word."

"You're asking me to be like a white knight, riding to the rescue of a maiden in distress."

"I am asking you that."

And suddenly, Sam was looking at things differently. He'd been so consumed by his pain and his anger that he had not thought about her feelings.

Was Shelby in distress?

Of course she was!

There was no way what had transpired between them over the last few months was not the truest thing that had ever happened to both of them.

Buckie was right.

Sam was just plain dumb. The truth had been right in front of him all along. Somehow knowing it didn't make him any less angry with her.

CHAPTER TWENTY

SHELBY HEARD SOMEONE pounding on her apartment door. It matched the pounding in her head. She felt exactly as if she had a hangover, but she did not.

Unless emotion caused hangovers.

And then she deserved a doozy. After not remembering her mother for eighteen years, now it felt as if a dam had burst, and the memories would not stop coming, water pushing its way through every weak spot, rushing out.

Plus, she had just hung up from Hannah. She had done as she promised Sam she would. She had called every day for the first week. And then she'd eased off just a little bit. And now, three weeks after her father's birthday party, she was calling every third or fourth day. Usually she did a video call, but today she was pretty sure Hannah would have picked up on how hideous she looked.

So, she'd done a regular call. She'd sung *Old MacDonald*, she'd put extra enthusiasm into the oinking.

And she had hung up the phone and done what she did every single time she hung up the phone.

Cried.

She missed them so much. Hannah. Alvin. Rascal. She missed it all so much. Mouse pancakes and sprinklers and storybooks and games. She missed cows lowing in the distance, elk on the lawn in the morning, the cool, pure breezes coming from the mountains.

Sam.

Especially Sam.

She missed the look in his eyes, and his smile, his hair growing back in curly. She missed his hands: those beautiful, competent, strong hands that could fly a helicopter or throw a calf, and yet be so tender when holding her hand, or so on fire as they brailled her body.

She missed sharing worlds and jokes and ice-cream cones.

Shelby had not known until now that you could physically ache for a person, that you could want them so badly your teeth hurt, that you could feel a dark hole of emptiness inside of you that felt as if it could swallow you.

The pounding at the door came again.

It was unusual to get someone at her apartment door unannounced. Visitors to the building had to get by a doorman and a concierge.

She decided to ignore it, but it came again, insistent.

Maybe the building was on fire and they were ordering evacuation. Or a pervert had slipped in and he was going to tell her he needed to come into her apartment for some manufactured emergency.

She got up off the couch, padded to the door and threw it open, and didn't bother with the peephole. She thought, *Let fate take me.*

Shelby was stunned at where fate intended to take her. Sam stood there.

Sam. The relief she felt was intense, even as she tried to school herself not to show it. She was *saving* him. And Hannah. She could not throw herself against him, and wrap her arms around him, as if he was a knight who had arrived on his steed to save her.

Besides, nothing in his face invited that.

He looked furious.

Gloriously handsome, but furious.

Except for the night she had told him she was not really a nanny, she did not think she had seen Sam angry.

And this did not compare to that. It would be like comparing a campfire to a volcano.

He was a volcano, right now, on the edge of eruption.

There was something about a man who was furious, and doing his best to contain it, that was oddly enticing. Like that thunderstorm the night they had first made love.

She could not think of that right now.

"What the hell are you doing?" he bit out, his gaze raking her.

She realized she must look beyond horrible. Her hair tangled, her eyes puffy from crying, her uniform of sweatpants and an old T-shirt unchanged for days.

"What the hell are you doing?" she shot back.

He glared at her and pushed by her into her apartment. He stood there, looking around grimly. She saw it through his eyes. The curtains were closed. There were two empty ice-cream containers on the coffee table, and one half-eaten microwaved lasagna on a television tray.

He swung around and looked at her. "You tell me what's going on. Right now."

Sam was not making a request. He was giving an order.

Shelby closed the door, leaned against it, folded her arms over her chest.

"I told you what's going on," she said. "We had a great time. Loved every moment. But it was interfering with my career."

He cast another look around the apartment. "I can clearly see your career is a priority."

Don't break, she ordered herself, but she was breaking. It was as if she was full of cracks and his arrival was putting pressure on them, and they were opening. If she didn't get things under control, he was going to see how broken she was.

But, wait. That's what he needed to see. That she was way too damaged for him to want, for him to invite into his life, and the life of his daughter.

"The night of my dad's birthday party—"

"The night you left," he snapped.

"I asked him about my mom. I asked him why I couldn't remember her."

His whole expression changed. "What did he say?"

"You know why I didn't remember her, Sam? Because she didn't love me. She hated me. She hated every single thing about me. She hated being a mom."

For a moment, he stood there, absolutely frozen. And then in one long stride, he came to her, and his arms folded around her.

It felt as if she had been adrift on a raft in the middle of the ocean, hopeless, and the rescue craft had appeared.

It felt as if she had wandered, dying of thirst in the desert, and found an oasis.

It felt as if she had been lost in the deepest, darkest forest, and finally saw the light.

Of home.

That's what she felt as his arms closed around her. A sensation of being home.

If she would have had the strength she would have pulled away. But she had no strength left. She could not fight the relief of this: someone coming after her. She leaned into what he offered, and she wept. She had thought she had no tears left, but it turned out she did.

He lifted her easily into his chest, carried her to her sofa, sat down with her on his lap, stroking her hair, saying soothing things.

"Tell me," he said, and though his tone was more gentle than it had been before, it was still an order that brooked no argument.

"I can't stop remembering things. About my mom."

"Tell me."

She had not said a word about these memories to a single soul. It felt as if they were corrosive, eating away at her.

"I remember clinging to her leg as she was trying to get out the door to go to a party, and her prying my fingers from her slacks."

His complete attention was her antidote to the poison she had swallowed. She could feel the toxin within her dilute.

"I remember begging for a story and being laughed at. *Me? Do I look like I read stories? For god's sake, the next thing you'll want is a mommy who makes cookies.*

"I remember wearing my prettiest dress, wanting just to be noticed, just to be approved of, and her not even looking at me.

"I remember drawing pictures, signed with love

hearts, that were glanced at, then tossed away with no comment.

"I remember her promising to be there for things like the Christmas play, my kindergarten graduation and never showing up.

"I remember her telling me if I stopped *pestering* her, she'd take me shopping, or out for iced hot chocolate, or to the park. But she never did.

"I've waited and waited for you to disappoint me. I was nearly delirious with joy each time you kept a promise. But the trepidation would start to build for the next time."

One by one, Shelby told Sam every single thing she remembered. She thought she would feel deeply ashamed, weak for sharing these memories with him. But instead, as she spoke the dam emptied, as if all the dirty, debris-filled water had to be cleared away.

Until she came to the last one.

"I remember screaming I loved her at her as she headed out the door. I think I have believed, my whole life, even though I didn't remember saying those words, that saying them had the power to kill."

"The exact opposite," he said firmly. "Do you hear me?"

"Yes."

"Good."

But still, she did not say them. "So," she finally said. "You can see why I had to go."

"I don't, really. I don't get it."

"Oh, Sam, she's half of me. Those parts of her are in me. My own mother didn't love me. Who could love me?"

"I could," he said, softly, and with such conviction. "I think you're looking at it all wrong, Shelby."

"In what way?"

"You are part of her. But you're the best part. You're her good thing, her one beautiful, good thing that she gave to the world. I don't know if there's a heaven, but I bet if there is, the best part of your mom, the undamaged part, her soul, is looking down, saying *See? I made it. The best part of me survived. I go on, in my daughter, in that beautiful, strong, resilient woman who took everything I gave her, who took all that coal I heaped on her, and mined it for diamonds.*"

She could feel his words seeping into her, like warmed wine, thawing all the places she had turned to ice.

"What if you're wrong?" she whispered.

"I'm not wrong. I remember what Buckie told me the first day you were there."

"What did he tell you?"

"He said, anybody who can't tell who that girl is from lookin' in her eyes is just plain dumb."

"Buckie said that about me?"

"Day one."

"You do a pretty good Buckie impression."

"I know. Don't tell him."

A small bubble of laughter escaped her. Five minutes ago, she had thought she was facing a life without one more moment of laughter in it.

This had been the miracle of Sam from the very beginning: life having a different plan for her than she had for herself.

Thank goodness.

"I miss him. And I miss Hannah." She took a deep breath. "And you, Sam. I miss you so much. It feels as if my world has gone from full color to black and gray."

"I'm going to suggest something to you," he said quietly. "I'm going to suggest that what made you run away from us was not just remembering your mom.

"It was more than that. It's terror that love will let you down. That it will hurt you more than you can bear. That it will give something to you that you feel you can't live without and then it will snatch it away."

"That's you, isn't it? With Beth?"

He nodded. "It is. I'm terrified of this thing called love. But you know, when I was growing up, the cowboys taught me something. They taught me it's not courage if you're not afraid in the first place.

"Life, Shelby, is asking you and I to step up to the plate. To be courageous in the face of our terror. To say to that little girl we're going to raise together—with our actions as much as our words—that love is worth it.

"That love is everything."

"Love is everything," she whispered.

He slipped out from under her and got down on one knee before her.

It was a surreal moment. Her billionaire cowboy kneeling on a stained pizza napkin in front of her.

Sam slipped a ring box from his pocket and opened it.

There was not much light in her apartment, but what there was was captured deep in the facets of that ring and shone back out at her.

She could hear his voice saying, *Who took all that coal I heaped on her, and mined it for diamonds.*

Shelby was pretty sure she would hear his words, and the pure love in them every single time she wore this ring.

She stared at the sparkling diamond, and then at the sparkle that meant more to her than diamonds. The deep sparkle in his eyes.

Of strength. Honesty. Trust.

Love.

"I want you to marry me, Shelby Kane. I love you."

This then was life, too. He was right. Everything you cared about could be snatched away in a breath.

Wasn't that a reminder to make each breath count?

And as much as life could take things away unexpectedly, it also brought things unexpectedly. Her day had started with despondency and darkness.

And now she was here.

In bliss, in the Light.

She had to dig deep for the words. But when she found them, it was as if they had been waiting for her, a treasure chest buried deep, deep within her.

People said when you find yourself in a hole to quit digging.

But what if you quit before you found this? The treasure chest?

She reached tentatively for the chest. The lock on it opened beneath her fingers. The lid was heavy, and the hinges were rusted.

It took all her strength to do what she needed to do.

She opened the lid of the treasure chest within her. She was afraid, after all this time, it might be full of snakes, or monsters, or rot, or dust.

Instead, Shelby was almost blinded by the brilliance of what waited for her.

She said the words.

"I love you."

And her world did not fall apart. Just as Sam had predicted, the exact opposite happened. She could

feel her whole world—and her bruised heart—
sparkling like jewels, lit from within.

"Yes," she whispered to Sam, but also to the
whole Universe, "yes."

EPILOGUE

THE OLD BARN was filled to absolute capacity, the front and back doors thrown wide to let in the spring breeze. The early afternoon light drenched the space.

It was a year to the day that Sam had first seen Shelby, coming toward him, her heel digging deep into the dirt, his daughter shooting her with her Bobby-doll.

Sam stood at the front, on the raised dais that had been built for this moment, thinking, *This is what miracles look like.* He felt a shiver of pure wonder move up his spine.

Alvin stood beside him as his best man, and he glanced at him. Alvin looked surprisingly civilized in a black tuxedo, crisp white shirt, a neat bow tie, a clean new cowboy hat, boots that shone until they sparkled.

If Sam had been hoping for a shared glance that said Alvin, too, was feeling the utter enchantment of this moment, he was disappointed.

Without any change in the expression worthy of

such a solemn occasion, Alvin winked at someone. Sam followed his gaze. The Duchess—or Countess—of Chanterbury was blushing under her extravagant hat. She and Alvin had met at Boswell's birthday party.

Sam's gaze moved from her and swept the crowd. The barn had never hosted such a diverse gathering.

Every race was represented. Shelby's assistant, Marcus, was there with his partner, sitting shoulder to shoulder with Sam's ranch hand, Jimmy, and his soon-to-be wife, Sandra. They were all laughing about something.

There were celebrities, and some of the world's wealthiest people. There were his longtime business associates and friends from his university days.

The ranch community was out in full force. Ranchers and cowboys, their families, and the people who supported them, store owners and beef processors.

It was a meeting of worlds that should never have worked, and yet it *was* working. Looking out at that gathering, Sam felt as if he was having a little glimpse of heaven.

Joy hummed in the air.

This was the universal truth: everyone wanted love. The richest, the poorest, the most elevated, the humblest.

Whatever barriers usually stood between them

were erased. This was the meeting place where everyone seemed to recognize each other at the deepest level.

Love.

The music began. A single violin played *Canon* by Pachelbel. The music soared, and as if on cue, two bluebirds, a bright male and his quieter companion, flew in the open front doors, over the assembled, and out the back ones.

Then Hannah appeared. She was wearing a pale blue dress made of lace and chiffon. Her hair had a band of wildflowers around it, but was loose and curled wildly around her flushed face. She was practically dancing down the aisle in her pink cowboy boots, scattering the wildflower petals that she and Shelby had gathered the day before.

Other violins joined the solo, and here *she* came through those open doors.

Shelby. The woman who had given him back his heart by taking it. Completely.

Her father was escorting her, and she was absolutely radiant. Her white dress was simplicity personified, like something a goddess would wear: a fitted lace bodice, with a deep V-neckline, tight at her tiny waist and then the long silk skirt flaring out, flowing behind her.

Every now and then, Sam would catch a glimpse of her pink cowboy boots, purchased specifically to match Hannah's.

Shelby's hair, like Hannah's, was loose, a band of braided wildflowers encircling her brow. The wildflowers matched her bouquet.

Her shining eyes saw only him. She arrived at him just as the music stopped, and they faced each other. He met her gaze, and everything else faded.

The barn. The light. The people. Alvin. Even his daughter.

In the clearness of Shelby's eyes, Sam saw the future. It was breathtaking. He saw babies and community, he saw Christmas trees and socks on the mantel. He saw a life that blended adventure and discovery with a place of safety and sanctuary.

When he looked in her eyes, he knew they had found the place the whole world longed for.

The place that love led one man and one woman, who had found each other against impossible odds, unerringly toward.

Home.

They had found home.

* * * * *